"ACCURSED BE HE WHO PROPHESIED THE KING'S DYING SO EVILLY AND SO WELL..."

That day in 1559 began ill-omened and I should have known its meaning. From where I stood I could see the Queen's troubled face. The book lay on her lap, the page was marked:

The Young Lion shall overcome the Old
By a single duel in a martial field
His eye shall be rent in a Golden Cage
Two wounds from one, the cruel death is sealed

The King had already completed two rounds of the joust. He spurred his mount across the tourney field. As he angled his lance for the encounter, a sun-shaft struck the King's helmet like molten gold. Nostradamus's prophecy was about to come true.

VAGABOND PROPHET

A NOVEL OF

Nostradamus

& HIS TIME

ALLENE SYMONS

AVON
PUBLISHERS OF BARD, CAMELOT, DISCUS AND FLARE BOOKS

VAGABOND PROPHET is an original publication of Avon
Books. This work has never before appeared in book form.

Cover illustration by Wayne Barlowe

AVON BOOKS
A division of
The Hearst Corporation
1790 Broadway
New York, New York 10019

First Avon Printing, September, 1983

AVON TRADEMARK REG. U. S. PAT. OFF. AND IN
OTHER COUNTRIES, MARCA REGISTRADA, HECHO EN
U. S. A.

Printed in the U. S. A.

WFH   10 9 8 7 6 5 4 3 2 1

FOR WANDA

VAGABOND PROPHET

PROLOGUE

I Alain Saint-Germain, am not given to prophetic visions. Only once in a childhood dream did I catch a single future glimpse: in that dream I saw the garden of Michel de Nostredame mobbed by an angry crowd who held aloft the charred effigy of a man. A terrifying vision, but one diminished by daylight and soon forgotten—until a June day many decades later.

I recall it clearly, the dream and the day; the smell of burning rags and timbers, the voices of men crying out for revenge. Odd, how memory in an old man is snared by a sound or a scent such as the innocent embers that warm me on this last day of the old year.

Journals, yellowed and torn, lie on the slab table before me; beside them, a few rare letters from my friend, Michel. Together they will goad me to the completion of this account, a task I have long intended to accomplish.

That June day in 1559 began ill-omened; why did I not suspect a tragic turn of event? Above the towers of Les Tournelles, heavy storm clouds marred the early sky, prelude to a wedding celebration which should have been blessed by sunlight, not shrouded in gray.

I recall that the weather made us all uneasy.

Queen Catherine reclined within her royal suite surrounded by bed drapes of vermilion satin. I had borne a message to her from the King and was told to wait, so I stood across the room and listened while the old Florentine chef confirmed his elaborate plans for serving peacock and other delicacies to a thousand guests. Many of them had traveled far to witness the sacred ceremony bonding two countries by the nuptial Mass, for Princess Elizabeth was to be joined with Phillip, King of Spain, and King Henri's sister, Marguerite, to Phillip's ally, the Duke of Savoy.

I watched as the dressmaker arrived with her assistants to display the narrow-thread lace which was added the night before to bridal gowns and trains. The Queen nodded approval but showed no sign of pleasure over the remarkable lacework, ordinarily one of her passions.

As one of the slashes on my shoe was poorly cut and bit into my foot, I shifted my weight. From where I stood, I could see the Queen's troubled face and knew more than dark clouds concerned her. She reached for the drawer-pull on her bedside stand and lifted out a book in which lay a fringed leather marker. She placed the book on her lap, unopened. I knew the cited page well and the quatrain which Catherine had set to memory:

> The Young Lion shall overcome the Old
>   By a single duel in a martial field
> His eye shall be rent in a Golden Cage
>   Two wounds from one, the cruel death is sealed.

You will need no interpretation now that fact stands in place of prophecy, yet remember that on that morning Nostradamus's words remained unfulfilled. In those days, one did not take such predictions lightly; his forecasts too often had proven true. And though each quatrain was cryptic, this one was clearer than most; thus Catherine interpreted King Henri to be the Old Lion but she puzzled over the place and time of death in a martial field, for those were times of peace.

After the long wait, my foot threatened to numb. I cleared my throat to see if the Queen had forgotten me. Startled, she looked up then told me to go, I was not needed. While taking my leave, I saw her replace *The Prophecies* in the drawer and remove a kidskin pouch containing a moonstone. She held it between a thumb and two fingers, rubbing the milky agate slowly, for someone once told her the stone would ward off sadness.

By late morning, as the appointed hour of the tournament drew near, the canopy of clouds parted and ladies no longer worried for their frocks. The jousting tourney was the only nuptial event held beyond the walls, on the Rue Saint-Antoine. It was an exercise in honor favored by the King and welcomed by guests who otherwise would spend three days feasting to the point of bilious agony.

For their comfort, wooden scaffolds of as many as three tiers had been built around the perimeter of the field. All seats were hung with bright flags or festooned with colored bunting. When the sun reached its apogee, the streets lay nearly deserted, but the scaffold seats brimmed with spectators. Upon rooftops, from windows and over the tops of turrets for a great distance around the field, you could see clusters of men and women, all waiting to view the traditional mock battle.

As the wedding ceremony glorified the brides, the tournament was staged to enhance King Henri's magnificence. For this monarch, facing his forty-first year, the tourney alone was reason to spend several thousand ducats. But his money's worth was not to be had sitting comfortably in the royal stand, reviewing captains who had already won glory on the battlefield.

With aid from his grooms, Henri mounted his steed. It was a proud white creature familiar with the weight of a man and full armor, but today burdened also with a chestpiece fashioned of silver on scalloped, tasseled brocade. Beneath the tassels it reared and stamped its hooves, raising columns of dust around its snowy fetlocks.

Henri jabbed his jeweled shoe into the horse's flank and sent it trotting heavily toward the point of combat. Two pairs of trumpeters blew six shrill notes into the air, stilling conversation in the stands. All eyes followed the King as he passed the tier where his mistress, the Lady Diane, sat serenely in a black and white gown that belied two decades of widow's mourning. The King paused below and lowered his helmet in her direction, then he turned the horse abruptly and rode to a halt beneath the royal stand. The Queen leaned forward in her seat, appearing as if to speak, but instead she threw him a rose that she plucked from the air and thrust beneath a flap of leather on his saddle.

Applause rose from the throng, approval of Henri's perfect form in the spirit of the day's match, for it promised no winner save the King. To unseat him would be unconscionable.

The tourney began, and in three artful sweeps of the wooden wall, the Duc de Guise lost to Henri. The duke's lance touched lightly upon the royal armor then veered off and jammed into the wall with a crack we could hear even above hoofbeats. It was a grand exhibition to see the monarch in combat, parrying his weapon with power and elegance, and I imagined that few spectators appreciated the challenge to his opponents, for their mastery of the lance was exceptional—that of men who could succumb yet leave an impression of hard-gained royal victory.

Between the first and second tilts, murmuring in the stands began again. Servants threaded through the rows with fans to cool the ladies, for now the June heat was bearing down through a patchy, clouded sky. Attendants rushed onto the field to clear away remnants of the duke's broken lance. Potholes in the course were turned smooth with iron rakes.

Then the second round began. The Duke of Savoy rode against the King. The duke was an excellent rider who adeptly maneuvered his own defeat and drove his roan as if life depended on the contest's outcome, delving his spurs into the roan's flank and sending the beast into great, lumbering strides. A fine act!

(I do not mean to slight the King's effort. A joust is

no mean feat, and he was no doubt as tired as his mount, with its foam-stippled coat).

As the King's third lance broke on the duke's arm guard, the crowd cheered thunderously, thinking this last pass marked the end of the exhibition, but in the din of applause Henri stood up in his stirrups, waved his hand high in a sign of endurance and sent his groom across the field to an officer named Montgomery, Captain of the King's Scots Guard.

I looked to the stand where Mary, the beautiful Queen of Scots and daughter of King James, sat beside the Dauphin, Henri's son. The girl smiled encouragingly toward her countryman Montgomery, though the prince at her side frowned with concern. Montgomery himself seemed surprised that the King would engage in yet another contest; three rounds would exhaust a far younger rider. But no one was empowered to curb his excess, and in short order a fresh horse was led alongside. Henri waved it away then spurred his mount across the tourney field into position at the end of the wooden barrier that separated combatants during the pass and prevented a collision between oncoming horses.

Montgomery rode to the opposite end and angled his lance for the first encounter. The King urged his horse into a heavy gallop along the wall, aiming his weapon for advantage, his weight forward as was the King's usual style before a parry. The plumes adorning his silver headpiece sagged from accumulated dust.

As the King and his captain closed in on the testing point, a sun-shaft broke through the clouds and struck the King's helmet like molten gold. I heard Montgomery's lance break against the King's armor and watched in horror as the tip of the lance splintered into deadly prongs and knifed sharply through the King's visor.

Henri dropped the reins, slid forward onto the horse's neck and clasped the beast desperately with one arm until from habit the horse slowed near the end of the course, blood streaming down its neck.

The crowd stood; the field filled with men, and someone stopped the beast in time to catch its falling rider. They tore off the silver helmet, and I could see no more behind the throng until a litter arrived and they carried the King away.

That night, the populace stood in vigil beyond the walls of Les Tournelles. Some held hope for the King's life, but they were mostly old women who knelt before the palace gates and loudly wailed prayers, expecting a miracle. The others did not wait to mourn, and soon their grief turned to anger. I keened my ears to the din below and from the milling crowd I heard a vengeful cry: "Accursed be he who prophesied the King's dying so evilly and so well!"

With a fear and a certain fascination I considered slipping into the crowd like Nostradamus's curious double, but I knew what I would see, and that I would only return stinking of smoke but be no wiser for watching ignorant *cabans* banking their pyres.

Instead I raged inside myself at the hypocrisy of men who clamored in the marketplace for copies of *The Prophecies*, those who paid coins for truth yet cared only for the fantastical, and when the words were fulfilled, cursed Nostradamus for his verity. They did not understand the man, surmising he was a dealer in dark secrets. And yet I had long known him as a man of faith and high aspiration, a devoted husband and enduring friend.

In an earlier and simpler time when we talked blithely of our futures, I had spoken of writing poetry in the hope that one day my name would be known across this land—yet Michel was the one who had attained fame through his quatrains; no, he had embraced infamy. And so monstrous was my countrymen's misconception of him on that night that I vowed, as I stood on the balcony with smoke stinging my eyes, to someday tell the true and entire tale of Michel de Nostredame.

Finally, I am disposed to do it, to capture his life in words. I call upon memory and imagination to aid me when the journals and letters provide an insufficient record, but I will be forgiven this liberty by anyone who has read Michel's work, for they will already know: a poet's truth is not the same as everyman's.

I

CONCERNING THE PATHWAYS TO PROPHECY

IN our natal village of Saint-Rémy, when my tutor had gone and my daily tasks were done, I would run along the cobbled streets with sandals striking against unyielding stones until I reached Michel's home on the Rue de Barri. Recalling those years conjures forth a courtyard garden where boxwood hedges neatly portioned off the vegetable garden and where vines of morning glory sprawled along ginger-colored walls; where olive trees and flowering plum offered shade and new grass thrust up bright spires from the moist, dark sod.

Behind the garden was a solidly built storage room with walls thicker than those of the living quarters. Michel's father, Jaume de Nostredame, had constructed it with raised slat floors to protect the grain from dampness, and it had openings beneath the eaves, set at an angle, to allow ventilation yet prevent driving rains from spoiling his stores of barley, millet and wheat. It was an unusual granary, and I have seen none like it since; thus was the family of Michel de Nostredame ever inclined to originality.

Michel had four brothers, but only he showed an early gift for scholarship, and therefore he was exempt from toiling in his father's trade. The family expected their eldest son to study medicine, and to this end he was instructed daily by his grandfather, Jean de Saint-Rémy, who was himself once a physician.

Our families were bonded by membership in that rising class of merchants among whom gold replaced the fraternity of noble blood. Yet within the brotherhood of merchants there were distinctions.

In those days, Michel's family was not as wealthy as mine, but Jaume de Nostredame provided his wife and children with a comfortable home and they suffered no lack. They owned their dwelling and the adjacent land housing the granary, and Michel's father did a steady trade in grains. Michel's mother, Reneé, was a frail woman with serene gray eyes she had passed along to her eldest son. It was in part due to her health and his devotion to her that Jaume de Nostredame rarely ventured forth on buying trips and instead relied on his assistant to procure the goods which he sold throughout Provence. His concern for Michel's mother, and for his sons, gave Jaume a stern countenance. He was nonetheless a kind and generous man but, like my own father, very practical.

Their home was not large, but solid and well-crafted. In the warming room—the kitchen—table and chairs glowed from careful polishing. Gleaming brass utensils and bundles of onions and herbs hung from beams set into the whitewashed walls, and always there was ample and excellent food prepared by Reneé with the help of a serving girl.

Our homes were similar in appointment, though mine was larger as befit my father's income; I had an entire small room to myself while Michel had a cozy storage space up a ladder off the kitchen.

Our land of Provence was the home of troubadours who many years before my time had spread their tales of heroes and fancy. But I have Michel's family to thank for my own interest in scholarship and for the love of words that set me on my own course, for my own family set less store by learning, and as I grew older I had to convince them that to have an educated son (for I had but one sister) would befit the family's increasing stature.

Michel's family needed no convincing of the importance of education, and indeed my friend was naturally gifted in languages and mathematics. As a boy he studied with his learned grandfather, and I recall the day that I stumbled onto the great difference between our two families, a difference of which I had only heard my parents whisper...

It was a sunny April day in the year 1518. Michel's grandfather had carried his cherished books into a corner of the garden, where he was instructing Michel in the writings of the Hebrews, the Romans and the Greeks.

I arrived unnoticed and decided not to disturb them. I spied a soft mossy place behind a tree and sat there, out of view, to wait for the conclusion of Michel's lesson. The sun was past the high point of noon, and I knew the old man usually closed his books when the sun reached the top of a certain olive tree in the garden.

"Grandfather," Michel asked, "is the *apeiron* of Anaximander the same as the *olam* of the Hebrews?"

The old man paused, then answered cautiously: "*Olam* means boundless time, an endless time which stretches ahead and into the past, but Anaximander writes of extension without end; to him *apeiron* means boundless space."

"But if they are both without limit, then why are time and space not one?"

"Wise men say this is so, yet our words bind us with limitations." The old man sighed, his eyes wandering skyward toward the light-rimmed clouds. I wondered if at last he was losing his celebrated faculties, but no, he was merely preparing to bait his grandson into argument.

"Michel, do you know why I wish to conduct our lesson in the garden today?"

Michel replied curtly, "No, for I am a better pupil in the house where I'm not distracted by sun and moths."

His grandsire countered, "But do you find no beauty in this day?"

"Springtime makes men into fools," said Michel, then, regretting his disrespectful tone of voice, he added, "Wouldn't Plato agree that we only see shadows thrown on walls, dancing images to seduce us from truth?"

I sat beneath my tree and listened to this sober side of Michel; it lay beyond my understanding. Michel and I were an unlikely pair. He was inclined to play solitary games or to labor over his books, but not I. Convincing him to join me in my countryside explorations required an immense effort, and when I finally persuaded him, he carried along his ever-present notebook and jotted down his observations, curious only about the oddities and flaws of nature.

"You misinterpret Plato's words," said the grandfather. "Beauty need not lead you from truth, but in it you may glimpse the greater Form which lures you toward itself. Tomorrow you shall again read the *Symposium,* and this time know Plato's mind on the meaning of the beautiful."

I heard Michel grumbling over the assignment, for I knew that while he loved his studies, he was looking forward to the next morning when he had been promised a taster's part in the preparation of the season's first quince jam. Even now, huge baskets of fruit were piled in his mother's kitchen, awaiting the homely alchemy which would transform them into Michel's favorite delicacy; indeed, my friend was easily seduced by the wonders of the palate.

But when he began to speak out in defense of his long-awaited day, the grandfather silenced him. I peeked out to see the old man gathering smooth stones from the garden and eleven twigs, one longer than the rest.

"Think of these rocks and branches as the Tree of Life..."

I thought: stones and bark could never make a tree, in God's nature.

"...know that these materials before you have no content, no place in time. Tomorrow they may symbolize flesh; you may yet recognize them one day as a trial of your conscience. No thing is as it seems to he who forbids time and place to bind him, a man whose homeland can be marked on no map."

The old man took a breath and said slowly, "It is time to talk again of the Mysteries, and of your heritage."

This sounded like foolishness to me, even though the old man's voice was strangely compelling. Were these mysteries and the arrangement of garden debris the elements of some dark magic? I had often heard tales: Michel and his family were of the faith, or did it only seem so? My parents had once told me that Michel was a Jew. Michel and his grandfather did not know I listened as they spoke, yet now I stood as witness while the old man drew my friend into some strange rite. Apparently the teacher of Greek, Latin and mathematics had another purpose up his sly old sleeve.

For a moment I was afraid, fearing my soul would shrivel for being a bystander. But why should I anticipate evil? Perhaps this was only another kind of faith, odd-appearing to an outsider. And if I thought about it, wasn't my own faith peculiar? Even I became confused when I paused to consider the mystery of an omnipotent God who could somehow reside in the temporal body of a man, His Son.

"Mi-ka-el," the old man intoned, "your namesake was leader of the Tribe of Issachar, the accursed ones who bought comfort and peace by wearing the yoke of captors rather than choosing the lean freedom of their faith. Do not forget this lesson in weakness. Listen for a sign from your heart."

At that moment from my mossy spot behind the tree, I sneezed. Crimson-faced, I leaped from behind the olive tree and tried to appear as though I had just arrived through the garden gate.

Michel sprang from the ground and stared as the old man destroyed his emblem with the quick sweep of a gnarled hand.

"Draper's boy, why do you hide?" asked the old one, seeing through my ploy.

"I did not wish to disturb Michel's lesson," I replied, and then blurted out, "I have read the *Symposium*, too!"

He seemed puzzled by my presence, but just then

Michel's father and youngest brother walked into the garden.

"Is my son learning his lessons, Father?" asked Jaume de Nostredame. "I expect him to be ahead of his schoolmates when he attends medical college. We have carefully set aside money for his medical education at Montpellier, and I pray that our investment will not be wasted."

"His progress with the classics is remarkable," said the grandfather. "Even at his age, he asks questions which give me pause. His curiosity is insatiable."

I saw a frown cross the younger man's brow, as though the old man's remark caused concern. I had often seen a faraway look in the eyes of Michel's grandfather, yet in his father's eyes one saw only a shrewd immediacy, as though in the modeling of this characteristic God had skipped a generation by passing the distant gaze directly from grandsire to grandson.

"I hope you are not wasting your time on fables or spurious texts," said Michel's father, "for the boy already has an overdeveloped imagination, and his mother and I would suffer if he wasted his true gifts."

The old man smiled to himself and said, "Rest assured, I shall impart to him only those lessons which shall further his gifts. Now I notice that the sun has reached the top of the olive tree and it is time for my afternoon nap. These old eyes are sharpest in early light, and the draper's boy waits for Michel and Jean to join him in some afternoon adventure."

At last we set out for the plain, the three of us running across rain-puddled paths and glistening moss. At first little Jean and I followed at Michel's heels in an unspoken hierarchy of leadership. Jean and I chattered and shoved at each other, often oblivious of our direction, while Michel was quietly observant and sure of the way, as always.

Michel was not tall, but sinewy and compact, with olive skin, dark gray eyes, and a manner of staring into the distance which often gave the impression that he was sullen and restless. He was strong and self-assured, even haughty at times, and more than once I bore the brunt of his withering disdain. But on that day the recriminations were aimed at the little brother whose eyes darted and glanced about, delighted by the teeming woods. Michel was intolerant of the boy's light-hearted spirit; unfairly he regarded young Jean as a simpleton foolishly enchanted by the colorful tokens of the birthing season.

We walked through patches of blossoming broom and huddled groups of cypress, I abreast of Michel, until suddenly we became aware that one pair of footsteps was missing, which could only mean that Jean had dropped even farther behind than his usual dawdling third place. We stopped and turned to see the boy crouched over a large rock, watching something move across the sun-washed surface. Michel called out with an older brother's severity as he ran toward Jean, who with a mischievous grin raised a muddy-booted foot and thrust it full force onto the unsuspecting creature slithering across the rock.

"Idiot!" Michel cried, posing his hand for a strike and sending Jean scurrying into the bushes. Ignoring his little brother, Michel stared at a thin green snake lying limp upon the rock. Its head was crushed by Jean's boot heel, but the rest of the reptile's body remained unmarred. Michel retrieved it by the tail, dangling the serpent from his fingers like a green and silver cord. As his anger turned to interest, Jean and I cautiously approached to take a closer look while Michel took out a notebook and began to enter his observations.

"How flat it is," said Jean quizzically. "Why was it rounded like a pipe before I killed it? Was it full of air?"

"Muscles made its shape, like those in your arm," Michel replied, continuing to write. Then he lay the notebook on a nearby stump and grasped his brother's arm.

"Ouch!"

"I was only pointing out your muscle. Grandfather says that in his day the Church forbade students to open the bodies of the dead for study of muscles and organs."

"You will be a great physician like your grandfather someday," I chimed in, praising the profession and reminding Michel that one of his forebears had been physician-in-attendance to King René of Provence. I did not add that my parents said the legendary doctor had been no blood relation to Michel's family.

"If my father has his way I shall be swabbing wounds and treating sores. But if I have *my* way I shall not live in Saint-Rémy and my profession will not be physicking."

Michel threw the lifeless snake into a nearby stand of cypress, casting it high into the air. We waited for the inevitable sound of impact on soggy earth, but there was only the soft drone of insects. Jean and I glanced at each other and, united by curiosity, we headed into the clearing to solve this mystery. Soon I found the snake, draped across a jagged bough; it never reached its destination.

Michel had lapsed into a moody melancholy and continued to sit where Jean had crushed the snake. Jean picked up a stone and heaved it as far as his small arms allowed. A brook flowed nearby and I proposed that we have a skipping-stone contest, but no amount of entreating would move Michel, and so the younger boy and I set off alone, promising to meet Michel later in the clearing.

"How long have I been sitting here?" he asked when Jean and I joined him for our walk home. "I've had the strangest reverie, and thought I was looking at the clouds for only a short while, yet I can see that it has grown late."

He was silent as we returned to the village along a stretch of gently sloping roadway until, at a curve in the road, Michel stopped and stood still as a column. I stood across from him and followed his gaze toward the ground, where rivulets of rain had etched delicate, spectral patterns into the tawny soil. To me it was a pretty pattern, but nothing more. But what did Michel see that stopped him so suddenly? How could he gaze at a cloud for over an hour? His eyes now seemed without focus as he looked downward, yet I had seen him stare at simple things strangely before and I never asked him why.

"We should be going," I said, but he gave no answer

and did not stir, as though in all the world he stood alone.

He closed his eyes; I saw his eyelids quiver and, thinking he might be ill, I took his arm. "Leave me," he whispered, and opened his eyes again. Whatever they saw, it must have been beautiful and awesome, for that look on his face I will never forget, yet all I saw before us was a mound of earth. Then I noticed that little Jean, who loved to disturb nests and burrows or any other order in nature, was ready to leap upon the knoll. I quickly bribed him away by offering to play a game of toss in his garden before dark.

We threw a stuffed-leather ball back and forth during the next hour while the sun fast descended toward the rim of the garden wall. Even as we began our game, the waning light allowed us only half a ball court. Many times I groped in the shadowed hedges after the ball, pricking my fingers on rose thorns. I finally announced the last toss and turned the ball in my hand: a dozen stitched pieces of hide forming the playful dodecahedron. But before I could throw, the gate swung open and Michel appeared, partly hidden by the shadow-darkened wall. He drew near, then clasped my wrist in a powerful grip. A chill of fear coursed up my back when I looked into his gray eyes and recognized the same smoldering gaze that once I had seen in the eyes of a wandering madman.

Then, as suddenly as Michel had appeared, he abruptly turned and walked into the house, with little Jean running close behind.

The next day when I arrived at Michel's home in the afternoon, he met me at the gate.

"Alain, I cannot join you today nor for a long while. My father insists that I go to a new tutor to study those lessons which will lead to my medical education. Though he will not know this, I shall also go to my grandfather's house every afternoon for other studies. He is expecting me now ... but please, trust in me and in our friendship."

I walked with him as far as the road leading to his

grandfather's house, where he turned to me and said,
"I must ask you a great favor: share my lie, for Father
will think I am with you each day."

"If you wish," I said sadly, then asked when I would
see him again.

"On Sundays, at Mass," he replied, and we went our
separate ways.

Unlike Michel, I had no brothers to turn to for com-
panionship, but only a sister whose constant simpering
made my life miserable. I could not tell my mother, who
bustled about the kitchen, the reason for my ill humor,
for now I was part of Michel's conspiracy. Our home
seemed gloomy that afternoon. A storm was gathering,
and inside the gray light made the polished tiles of my
mother's floor look sad and dull. Even the smell of bak-
ing bread did nothing to warm my spirits.

During the next two years I saw Michel rarely, and
in the afternoons when my own tutoring was done, I
turned to a journal that I had begun, and in my solitude
I found comfort and amusement by trying to capture
impressions in verse. Some days, when I was restless
or when my father insisted, I would work in my father's
shop, sorting heavy bolts of broadcloth, silk, linen and
wool. My arms grew stronger as I heaved the bolts from
floor to storage rack with energy born of a still-linger-
ing resentment toward Michel, who had cut me out of
his life and yet expected me to support his lies. We only
spoke briefly on Sundays, after which he would call
loudly, for all to hear, "See you tomorrow," though of
course he never did.

Then, toward the end of the second year, the old man
died; three weeks later Michel reappeared at my doorway carrying a book in his hand.

"Alain?" he said hesitantly. "May I come in?"

With a chilly reserve intended to shield me from
further disappointment, I motioned for him to enter.
My father was traveling in search of goods to buy cheaply
and sell dear; it was his guiding principle, and one I
wished not to emulate. I offered Michel the high-backed

chair usually occupied by my father. By this formality, he sensed my displeasure.

"Is our friendship so easily lost?"

"I have done the favor you asked," I replied flatly.

"Alain, my decision two years ago was not a simple one, and now I grieve and come to you for help. I grieve for the loss of my grandfather, and no one but you knows the nature of our secret pact. I somehow thought the sharing of that secret showed my trust, but perhaps I have assumed too much."

My sulking suddenly struck me as childish; first I grinned, then we both began to laugh.

"It is good to smile again," he said, handing me the book. "I've brought a gift—a new edition of François Villon."

I ran my fingers over the book of poetry, across the rich binding and embossed title letters tooled in gold.

"I purchased it last week in Lyons," he said, his eyes bright. "I wish you had been along, Alain, to see the wondrous yield of the printer's craft. Just thinking of the power of printed words brings an ache of excitement to my head."

I thanked him and turned the pages, fine sheets of soft rag paper printed in the newest style of type.

"You were often on my mind," he said cautiously, as if still unsure of my acceptance. "You would have laughed to see me rummaging through the books like a person possessed—all to my father's dismay, for he fears I do not have a properly stable temperament for a student of medicine."

"My father has gained little confidence in me these past two years either," I confided. "He calls me a dreamer and has only disdain for what he calls my 'scraps of rhyme.' He says I have no business mind, and that I even confuse woof and warp. Worse, he cannot stand my lute, so I have to play it away from the house."

"You see," he said, "my absence has been of some benefit."

Michel was right. The journal had become my companion, and many of its pages contained new poems.

"What will happen to your education, now that your grandfather is gone?" I asked.

"I shall go to Avignon, where I will board with my cousins starting in the autumn term."

"Michel, this is a wonderful coincidence! I too am going to study in Avignon, though I will live in student lodgings." I added, "Our fathers have great plans for us; I hope we won't disappoint them."

Michel and I sat across from each other, relishing the renewed spirit between us and the anticipation of our student life ahead. But nothing further was said about friendship and its near loss, for it is fragile and does not bear well the weight of discussion.

* * *

That summer was hot, sweet with the scent of garden herbs, and our days seemed more precious with the knowledge that soon we would both leave home. As the season passed, I helped Father in his shop and for the interim Michel continued to study Latin with his tutor. Many afternoons, restless, we walked together through the countryside and talked of how our lives would soon change. Then, one day, I devised a game.

"Test your logic on this," I said to Michel. "Take as your starting premise a statement about some villager—say, his standing in Saint-Rémy. Then I challenge you to deduce his youth. What were his dreams, his ideal of love?"

Michel raised his brow in a response I recognized as interest. At once, he named a greedy baker whom we both knew well. "Today we see Jules Fenelon at sixty years of age. He is blind in one eye but otherwise healthy. From this we infer nothing," Michel said, shrugging. "But judging by the miserly manner in which he operates his pastry shop, and considering his wife," Michel grinned, thinking of the huge woman who must weigh at least eighteen stone, "I infer that Fenelon's ideal was to marry *une grande dame,* to entertain royally with servants heaping delicacies upon his notable guests. But alas, dreams have a way of turning upside down and sideways, like light in a prism."

I chuckled at his account of Jules Fenelon, which Michel delivered with mock gravity. Seeing my amusement, he proceeded to give "histories" of other townspeople. His ingenuity seemed endless, and only when he realized that it was past time for the midday meal did Michel abandon the game.

His considerable talent for playing my game was at first surprising, for I had never thought of Michel as possessing a sense of humor or as being given to fanciful thoughts. When I remarked on this, he said, "Ah, but you forget I've had training. Such fanciful thinking is at root logical, as you supposed when you told me to 'test my logic' on Jules Fenelon. It only requires notice of a man's present vices, then a turning back to earlier times. Add a touch of what my grandfather would have called Socratic irony, and you have the amusing effect."

I wonder, now, about those last months in Saint-Rémy. We idled away our afternoons for the last time, yet we found no time for girls. Were all our feminine acquaintances betrothed? Among those girls who were, shall I say, "within our reach," the daughters of lowlier families, did neither of us find temptation?

Perhaps the answer lay in my youthful shyness and in Michel's indifference, for I recall gazing in secret at beautiful girls but could find no corresponding longing in Michel.

Though our reasons were different, chastity may have been to our advantage. As my interest was merely in beholding a lovely girl from a safe distance while wooing her in my imagination, and as Michel was blind to girls altogether, neither of us had any lasting trouble due to the damsels of Saint-Rémy; neither wound up saddled with a young wife and babe, as did many of our more adventurous acquaintances.

Michel had once visited his uncle, aunt and cousins in Avignon where we were soon to begin our formal education. He described the city as one of "massive walls and a hundred towers"; however, from my father (who traveled frequently to that city), I learned that the towers numbered only thirty-nine. Michel likewise said that Avignon was still under papal control, though no longer the residence of His Holiness. And when I expressed interest in seeing the papal palace, to spare me disappointment my father warned me that it had fallen

into disrepair. He added that the return of the Pope to
Rome had in no way diminished Avignon's educational
program, considered one of the best in France, and only
a day's coach ride from Saint-Rémy.

We set out for Avignon on the last hot day of summer.
Our bundles of clothing and a few other belongings were
beneath our seats and beside us on the carriage floor.
I brought along a few volumes of poetry, which I intended to guard carefully, as the printed editions came
dear. I noticed, too, that Michel had a bundle which
appeared to be books, judging by the sharp corners visible beneath the burlap wrapping.

"Some are very old, written on delicate vellum and
I'd have to go far to replace them," he said over the din
of carriage wheels biting the ruts of a dry road. "They
were my grandfather's. Now they are mine."

The offhanded way he mentioned the old man opened
a topic which until then was forbidden by some unspoken agreement between us.

I ventured: "What *were* you studying those two years,
before he died? I've known no stranger moment in my
life than the day I left you standing by the roadside."

A dry gust of wind whipped through the coach window. Michel did not reply at first, and I feared I had
clumsily reopened a wound.

"Someday I shall tell you of that day," he said, turning to stare out the window, squinting into the sun.
"And yes, I would tell you of my grandfather's teachings, but only if you are sincerely interested."

I nodded, hoping I looked sincere rather than incredulous.

"My family is descended from Hebrews of the Tribe
of Issachar," he began. "It is an ancient and powerful
tradition. Before my birth, the Jews of Provence were
forced to decide between leaving their homes or con-
verting to the Church; my people chose to remain and
relinquish their faith, just as in Israel the Tribe of Issachar long ago chose to abandon their faith and remain
in comfort among captors."

"But the teachings you speak of," I interrupted, "they
have not been lost, for surely your grandfather taught

you everything he knew. What *were* those teachings, besides history and ancient languages?"

"It is impossible to tell of the teachings. They are like poetry, for poetry employs symbols; they are like logic, for from one truth another follows just as a conclusion may be implicit in the premises which precede it."

Our coach wheels hit a cavernous rut and sent our belongings sliding. Michel rearranged his and continued as though there had been no disturbance.

"In this secret study I was taught the art of such symbols and how to discover the linking of hidden truths. I was told in a vision that one day I would discover a grand chain of causes and consequences...that is all I can say, without risk of bewildering you."

"Do you now understand the old man's secrets?"

"No, I am more perplexed than before. There was so much to learn. After only one year he began to fail, though I tried to hear every word and to ask questions through all his waking hours. Even so, he gave me but a small portion of the legacy I was promised."

I often wondered when, if ever, Michel pored over his grandfather's books or practiced mysterious rites, the nature of which I could only guess. During the first weeks in Avignon I doubt if he had occasion even to unpack his burlap bag, so scarce was private time.

At first he resided with his younger cousins, but he complained so about the noisy, crowded house that within a few weeks he had joined me in the student lodgings. There, a rigorous schedule started at four in the morning when the proctor roused us from sleep. The earliest hour was always a blur to me, though Michel seized the darkness with teeth clenched in the cold, his brow set in an angry, determined frown. He jerked on his hose, doublet and black-belted gown and somehow was dressed and downstairs before I even began to pull on my leggings. Alone, I managed to find my way down the stairs and out the door, where I stood for a moment along with other students as we made water on the courtyard wall; it was somewhat a tradition.

After Mass was served and we had eaten our plain

hard rolls, the lectures began. The main class of the day was held earliest, when we were still alert. From ten to eleven we engaged in discussion and argument, then a succession of lectures occupied us the remainder of the day.

During the first year, Michel and I attended many of the same classes, suffering the discomfort of damp classrooms together, with our feet tucked into the straw that imparted a semblance of warmth to rooms otherwise bare but for benches and lectern.

One day while a professor held forth on the subject of Latin declension, I noticed Michel was drawing on the sheet of paper atop his scriptorium. He dipped his sharpened pen into the horn inkwell, then inscribed small figures into the margin of the sheet, interspersed with an occasional note from the lecture; indeed, the figures were so small that when the explorator passed by Michel's bench, he saw only the Latin notes in Michel's ordinary handwriting.

Now, I knew Michel had been studying astrology along with ancient languages, rhetoric and philosophy, and I recognized the marginalia as astrological symbols. It struck me as odd that he would be jotting them down so absentmindedly during a Latin lecture. Later, during our recreation time from two to three o'clock, I asked Michel about this.

"Let me ask *you* a question instead," he countered. "How do you fashion your poetry? In what moments do you compose?"

I replied that I felt almost compelled to write whenever a song arose in my head; moreover, I found fascination in the very urgency of this act, as though it came from another realm where Latin classes do not matter.

"Good," he said, "you've answered your own question, for what you've told me applies equally to the way I feel when I look upon a natal chart or horoscope. At first the task of learning planets and their attributes was tedious, as was mastery of the mathematical techniques for proper arrangement; yet after all this was accomplished, then I experienced what you have described: a burgeoning of ideas."

"Often the contemplation of some image or some external object releases the poetic urgency."

"So it is for me. After I study a horoscope for a time, I find my muse, as you would say, and I must note these ideas before they are lost. Sometimes it is most inconvenient, and they may continue to rise to the surface throughout the day. Even during Latin class."

"Now I understand you, Michel. Go on."

"Well, if I see in a natal chart that the planet Mars is in a malefic aspect to Neptune, I recognize a conflict between Mars's fiery nature and the depth of Neptune. Then for example if Mars is located in the Fourth House of domestic matters, I know the native of this horoscope is born with a temper likely to erupt near the hearth, along with abundant energy. Thus the hidden clues contained within the horoscope are revealed."

"Then astrology bears some relation to the symbols you were studying with your grandfather," I concluded.

"Yes, it is another branch of the same ancient tree. And now I know I shall never treat boils and broken limbs, Alain, for I have found my vocation. I have a gift for this study of the heavens—I am sure! Even the slightest understanding of planetary influence must be worth more than a thousand repetitions of the Mass."

Though Avignon was only a day's ride from Saint-Rémy, we were not encouraged to travel home by the stern Fathers who instructed us, and who (I suspect) wished to maintain discipline with as little interruption as possible. Nonetheless, Michel and I, like most of the students, did return home for Calendo, as Christmas was called in Provence, and to celebrate the Resurrection of Christ and birth of the New Year at Eastertime.

Thus it was on one of our visits home, at Eastertime in the year 1521, that my father began talking of his draper's trade as though assuming I would join him when my studies at Avignon were completed. I had no intention of undertaking his business, but did not admit this for fear he would make me leave school. Indeed, several of my schoolmates were in a like predicament, for this was a time when learning came into reach of merchants' sons who, once they had tasted the writings of Greece and Rome, were inspired to achievements other than shopkeeping and trading. In Michel's case, it was assumed that he would go on in medical studies, though I knew he was uncertain about such a path.

It was not until the following year, when we had completed our studies, that this problem came to the fore.

Now, I had never been as serious a student as Michel, but we did share a talent for memorization which I rarely used since the walled city offered subjects more exciting then the *trivium* and *quadrivium* or those humanistic subjects which comprised our coursework. In particular, I was drawn to a certain wine-purveyor's daughter whom I finally succeeded in bedding, though Michel remained indifferent to my accomplishment, such at it was.

On this note of triumph I concluded the year 1522, and returned home with a certificate of graduation.

My homecoming boded well, at least during the first few hours. Upon my arrival, while the carriage horses stamped impatiently and my parcels were being hoisted to the ground, I received warm embraces and congratulations from my parents and sister. My father was puffed with pride.

For the celebration dinner my mother prepared a delicious feast of lamb in wine and garlic with slices of olives shining in the broth like glistening black rings. But I must accept responsibility for a nasty turn in the afternoon's festive mood. After we had supped, I began to flaunt my knowledge of Greek and Latin poets; from this rather vulgar display of erudition it was a small step to proclaiming my chosen profession.

"Father, Mother," I announced loudly in a voice made bold by wine. "I, your son, will bring great honor to our family as a composer of verse!"

At this my father leaned forward in his chair, ready to dissuade me. "Wait," I said, raising my hand, "I am not the impractical dreamer you think, and I anticipate your objection. Poetry is not a sensible profession; thus, in order to earn a livelihood, I am prepared to work as a tutor."

"Your interest in classical poets is merely a fashion of our age," he argued. "It seems almost every man in the streets fancies himself a scholar and is determined to dredge up and translate 'lost' writings. Soon there will be a surfeit of desperate tutors and you shall all trade your services for a sou."

There was truth in his harsh assessment. A love of the antique had swept France since the campaign in Italy. Moreover, it was a pagan inspiration, some feared, and foretold a day when the very literature I hoped to teach would be proscribed by the Church. If so, I'd reap no benefit for all my trouble, and for my father's expenses of one hundred livres a year supporting my education.

"However," my father said pensively, "if you persist in this infatuation and take your lute-strumming seriously, perhaps you should consider an apprenticeship with a printer or a builder of musical instruments."

My boldness vanished and left me speechless, standing awkwardly before my half-eaten dish of lamb. I tried to clear my head and consider my position. He was offering me two choices, but this was only a ploy; no doubt he had already narrowed the field. "Which do you favor?" I asked. "The printing trade," he answered confidently, and added: "I will send a letter to your Uncle Léon. With his influence, he will find you an apprenticeship in Paris."

Though I suspected the letter had already been penned, I was neither delighted nor dismayed; in a haze of youthful optimism I believed other doors would miraculously open in welcome to my talents. But this was not all that buoyed my spirits. In that first two-year adventure away from home, I had discovered another skill which I was eager to practice, for after overcoming an initial shyness, I found I was naturally endowed with a certain ready geniality which had already earned me unexpected favors. As patronage came my way, so obstacles seemed to dissolve. And so, as my father stood before me awaiting a reply, I thought to myself: as long as I am in Paris, surely good fortune will not be far.

When I called upon Michel the next day, I found myself witness to another confrontation.

"I tell you, my life would be wasted prescribing tonics," Michel was saying to his father as I walked into the room. "Alain, here, knows of my devotion to astral studies," he said, dragging me into the situation, but I only nodded as Michel went on. "Father, you have no idea of my ability in what you call 'charlatanry.' My vision is a *gift*."

His father cut in, "Bah to your gift! Your great-grandfather had a gift as well, and not only was he physician to King René, but to common men."

Michel's father then proceeded to tell a story I remembered hearing in his home many years before: a moral tale, with the legendary physician as hero. It was the tale of a poor farmer's son who had been mauled by a boar. We waited patiently as Jaume de Nostredame built up to the final line: "... and your great-grandfather administered to the boy with such skill that beyond all hope the leg healed, and the boy grew to be a man who proudly tended his fields, instead of a pathetic cripple cowering in the streets—and all this due to the healing gifts of your ancestor."

Michel sighed as his father added a new ending to the litany, only for this occasion. "Furthermore," Jaume said, "I do not intend to support you in this folly. We have always expected you to attend the college of medicine at Montpellier. But if you insist on following the stars, you may gaze at them from the charity college of Montaigu where miserable food and lice will aid your meditations."

Michel inhaled deeply then faced me, and I knew by the defiant set of his mouth, the blade-gray chill of his eyes, that his decision was made: Montaigu. I dreaded the consequences for him. Michel was less robust than I, and the comfort of our childhood in Saint-Rémy had not prepared him even for the rigors of Avignon, much less for true hardship. From stories I had heard of the college of Montaigu, where classes were provided for poor but promising students, Avignon was idyllic in comparison. I feared the now-faint line between Michel's eyes would deepen into a bitter furrow; I imagined him hunched over a book in some cheerless, dank cell and stubbornly refusing to admit error and return home.

I lingered until his father had retired for the night; then, hoping to melt Michel's stiff-backed resistance, I cautiously suggested that he not risk the future by taking such a rigid stance. I offered him the following argument, founded upon the new philosophy of survival I had formulated the day before.

"Accept your father's offer," I advised. "Go to Montpellier and fulfill the medical requirements, yet at the same time pursue your own studies. It may take longer to complete the medical courses, but your father will not object—and he will not know you are dividing your time—just as he remained ignorant of your secret studies with your grandfather."

Michel cocked his left eyebrow; I had caught his curiosity. "You phrase this notion too neatly, as if I should spend one day studying anatomy and the next astral delineation."

"Allocate a few hours a day to each, as I will be doing," I said. "I've agreed to become a printer's apprentice, but I intend to spend every spare moment composing poetry and mastering my lute. I shall stretch myself into printer-poet-musician."

"Then I will be a success and you will be drawn and quartered by your ambitions," he said, laughing. I knew I had won.

"I should listen to your advice more often," said Michel. "Perhaps I see too distantly and ignore the facts in front of my nose."

He walked a short distance with me. The hour was late, the cobblestone streets dark and empty. He spoke with some envy of my forthcoming printer's apprenticeship and recalled the excitement he had known when perusing the books and pamphlets in Lyons. I turned in the direction of my home, wishing him a peaceful night, but after only a few steps Michel called me back.

"I will miss you, my friend; these have been good years together. I am grateful for your help tonight and for evoking the memory of my grandfather, for I believe he would bless the decision to study medicine and at the same time to continue my search."

"After all," I said, "your grandfather also followed a second and secret path."

Within a few months Michel was ensconced in the medical school at Montpellier, while I and my father had signed our names to a contract of apprenticeship with Gabriel Delille, printer.

I traveled to Paris in a coach surrounded by strangers, and though missing Michel at first, I soon caught the scent of independence. Without Michel's absorbing conversations, I would have more time to think for myself, to compose, to practice my lute; without his confining sense of morality, I would be primed to advance my finesse with women.

The first overnight stop proved a harbinger of adventures to come: the moment I entered the tavern, I saw a girl. She was perhaps a year or two younger than I, deliciously plump and rosy of cheek. She gave me a knowing smile and conducted me away from the other travelers who were vying for seats at a large plank table. Instead, she led me to an alcove by a wide oak cupboard and there served my supper in silence, except for a silken brush of her hand as she set out a plate of ham and lentils. I lagged behind until the others had departed for their rooms and Suzanne had finished her chores. Together we sat at a scrubbed plank table that smelled of soap.

She was lovely but unlettered. In the dim light of a single oil lamp, I confidently spun out stories of Avignon and found myself reciting to her long passages of classical poetry I'd almost forgotten. Before her admiring blue eyes, my memory soared. We walked softly upstairs to my room where I stroked the strings gently to a contented audience, and she lay beside me till sunrise.

Good fortune joined me for the journey to Paris, urging on my high spirits and affording safe passage. Then, as our coach neared the fabled city and began to traverse her outer bridge, I prayed silently and modestly to the Virgin: may this venture gain me a decent life and a few tender memories as consolation in later years. Then a gloomy notion clouded my prayer as I wondered: would the sum of my life consist of pretty tunes and frivolous souvenirs? I retracted the prayer at once, and before we had completed the bridge crossing I had made a firm resolve: I would devote myself to perfection of the poet's art, composing new works, each better than the one before; I would not squander myself on another poet's lines to win the favor of an impressionable girl.

In spite of my sincerity, I was to be tormented with temptations; they began with Monsieur Delille's wife.

Gabriel Delille was a meticulous craftsman and a miser. When I arrived at his home, struck speechless after my first ride through the city of Paris, he installed me in an attic room barely large enough for the small hard cot, a minuscule chest to hold my clothing and enough remaining floor space to set the lute precariously on end against my modest collection of books. To conserve space, I piled one book atop the next, forming a small tower of leather. Of course it was most inconvenient if I needed a book on the bottom of the pile. With this compact arrangement, a narrow strip of uncluttered floor led like a dwarf's footpath to the shoulder-high door.

After I had secured my belongings and had washed off the road dust with cool water from a chipped lavatory bowl, I descended the narrow stairs and landed on the ground floor to hear the rhythmic clash of metal striking against metal. I followed the noise until it drew me through a crude passageway between Delille's home and his printing shop, which filled the lower story of a small adjoining building.

I expected the press to be smaller, lower, a more tidy piece of machinery, perhaps because of the modest size of its product. There before me I saw a towering construction of black iron. The amazement on my face was plain. Delille laughed and offered me a skimpy mug of wine. "To my new apprentice," he said, tipping the pewter mug and emptying it in one gulp. He grinned slyly and with the wink of a beady eye added, "and to your uncle's influence—may it bring profit to us both."

I raised my mug and drained it to the dregs, which was not difficult, as I had been served a portion consisting of just that; nevertheless, it was bracing.

Delille gestured toward the press and said reverently, "It is fitting to drink a cup in her presence."

"Whose presence?"

"The printing press. Her forebears crushed grapes, but it took a clever, abstemious man to put a wooden block in place of grapes, and another clever man to think beyond a single carved block to the casting of separate letters so that type could be broken down and recomposed as another page."

"Formidable," I mumbled, relishing the bitter winy aftertaste beside the imposing black machine.

"Your Uncle Léon tells me you know nothing of printing," said Delille, "so I'll begin by explaining a few rudimentary points. First, apply water to the paper, for it increases the absorption of ink and produces a clearer printed page. You see, water is good for something besides irrigating the farmers' fields and washing soiled linen." He shook his head and added, "My wife thinks it beneficial to soak the body, but I regard it as a waste of time."

Thus far I had only seen his wife briefly, when I first entered the house with baggage in hand. But I did notice immediately that Madame Delille was a handsome woman scarcely older than myself. She modestly remained distant, not only the day of my arrival, but on the ensuing days as Delille imparted to me first the simple tasks, then the more complex. I am quick to learn, and presently I had mastered the essential techniques. I anticipated the day when I would operate the press alone; Delille insisted the day was far off. Pleasure in my labor had little to do with my impatience. I only sought to work one long day alone and to produce, hopefully by sunset, a page filled with my own verse.

But when my time came, it was denied. Delille was confined to bed with a severe chill. He swore I was not proficient enough to operate the press alone; nor had he strength to devise other tasks for me, so I was awarded a day at leisure.

An entire day to myself! In my mind I quickly divvied up my windfall of hours as though it were a pouch of coins, alloting a few hours for several coveted projects. First, I would spend the morning hours composing poetry; then, after a few hours exploring Paris (which I had seen only from my attic window except for the carriage ride to Delille's), I would devote the evening hours to playing my lute.

As I tallied these precious hours, I paused a moment to remember Michel, who by now was established in the Montpellier life. Self-satisfied, I hoped that he, too, had such occasional windfalls of time, and the ability to make shrewd use of them. Then I heard a tap on the door.

"Alain?" Madame Delille called faintly. "I have a letter for you."

"A moment," I replied, glancing quickly around the room to see if anything lay about which might give offense. I opened the low door; she smiled, looking beyond me into the room. My lute caught her fancy; her long-lashed eyes glittered.

"You are a musician," she said, handing me an envelope.

Respectfully I replied, "Yes, madame." But I should have been wary of her interest. Instead, I caught the spirit of the moment, not unlike casting dry twigs on a blaze, when I said, "And I also write poems meant to be sung to the instrument."

She assessed the room and wrinkled her nose slightly in disdain, though I could find nothing unpleasant and I had made every effort to keep my tiny cubicle clean.

"What a gloomy little hole he's given you," she said. "Join me downstairs by the fire. I'll listen to your songs— I've nothing special to do today."

I was tempted to answer, "Well, I *do* have other plans," but I thought as I was new in her household, it might be more prudent to please her, and agreed to join her in a short while.

When I could no longer hear her footsteps on the narrow stair, I removed the sealing wax with my thumb and unfolded Michel's letter.

From Montpellier, this tenth day of September in the year of our Lord 1523

My Dear Alain,

I find Montpellier to be most congenial to a beginning medical student of my temperament, for I have considerable freedom to observe and do value this time since later my work shall be watched more closely. For this reason I am keeping two sets of notebooks: one which may be examined by the doctors as a record of my studies, and a second, in which I inscribe my private and not always orthodox speculations.

Michel remarked that the city of Montpellier was pleasantly situated on the right bank of the small Lez River, dignified by the presence of a handsome cathedral built some hundred years ago.

He had already made the acquaintance of a small group of first-year students who gathered, somewhat clandestinely, to discuss matters discouraged by the Church, among them medical astrology. Michel explained that though natal tendencies were traditionally believed to have an influence on parts of the anatomy, lecturing physicians were also Churchmen and had "corrected" him when he phrased his questions in astrological terms. Michel commented one day about a patient with a lung disorder.

"A badly aspected Gemini Fourth House," Michel began.

"Saint Blasius is the patron saint of this organ," said the doctor sharply. "We do not speak in pagan terms here. You must learn to advise your patients to pray for appropriate intercession: Saint Erasmus for disorders of the abdomen, Saint Apollonia for the teeth and gums, Saints Lucia and Triduana for problems of the eye."

"Besides," another student added sarcastically under his breath, "if the treatment fails, then the appropriate saint shares the blame and your reputation is preserved."

Michel recounted this incident, among others, then closed the letter on a philosophical note:

Among the works I am required to read are, of course, the writings of Hippocrates. I leave you this thought from his *Aphorisms:*

Ars longa, Vita brevis

But no, I will give my translation in the vernacular, for I remember that you advocate use of the "living language" in which form this would read,

Life is short and the Art long
opportunity fleeting; experiment
dangerous, and judgment difficult

I agree with Hippocrates in all but one point; I would amend him to read "experiment is dangerous but essential, for by experiment our judgments become less difficult."

I smiled at Michel's boldness in presuming to improve upon Hippocrates, but now I clearly understood his reason for protecting private speculations. I folded the letter again, placed it in my traveling bag, and then remembered that Madame Delille awaited me downstairs. My heart contracted with worry over her intentions. Ah well, I thought, if Michel is correct, this experiment will ease the difficulty of future judgments.

Madame Delille stirred the smoldering fire with an iron, then asked me to set on another log. As the pungent bark gave light to the somber room, she motioned me to sit and then came close beside me, the hem of her gown covering my shoe. I placed my lute upon my knee; the notes melded with the sighing hearth. It was a ballad, familiar enough, that she began to hum softly.

"Play me a song of your own making," she said. I saw again the admiring look but foolishly chose to ignore it, drinking in her attention. My fingers danced across the strings with an excellence of timing and mood which surpassed what I had found in my finest moments.

"You should be a courtier, not an apprentice," she said. "You should be fitted out in velvet, not in cast-off aprons. Your talents are lost here."

Her hand lingered on my arm for the time of a slow breath, and I heard myself say in a stranger's voice, "Is he asleep?"

"Yes. The serving girl will return from her errand—but not soon."

Gabriel Delille remained in bed three days, but neither did I compose nor did I explore the streets of Paris. When we resumed our work at the press on a trebled schedule, with our sleeves rolled up and ink caked on our forearms, I often sensed that Françoise Delille was standing behind us. If I dared to turn, her unguarded green eyes sent messages of such unmistakable content that I was sure she sought discovery. In self-defense, I avoided her, only to be reprimanded by Delille for being *rude* to his wife.

"Forgive me," I said, thankful for his ignorance, "I've been intent on completing the work."

But when my eyes met her glance, my body tensed and my face became so miserably flushed that I knew I must take leave before the truth became known. Not only did I risk my livelihood, but also my life, for at times Delille had the temper of a crazed bear.

I had acquired some knowledge of printing in the past eight months. Surely my uncle, with his legendary influence, would have other contacts in the trade. But would he care to be bothered with me? Since my arrival, Uncle Léon had not so much as asked after my welfare. Not only was he aloof, but even if I succeeded in winning his sympathy, could he release me from the bond I had signed with Delille?

I sat in my small room that night contemplating my dilemma and vowing to the Virgin that in future I would keep my mind on business.

The next day I requested another day off, but Delille dismissed this wasteful notion, saying curtly, "The press should not be idle." Thus I resorted to trickery in order to wriggle out of an already unsavory situation. I offered a young boy a half-crown to deliver a message to me—from me, but signed Léon Saint-Germain. My Avignon education had left me with an elegant cursive hand, which adapted nicely to several distinctive styles of signature. I had yet the original copy of Uncle Léon's letter informing me of Delille's offer, and with little effort I copied his signature on a letter in which I stated that he was seriously ill and had requested my bedside presence as his kinsman. I added an afterthought: "As you play delicately and with considerable skill, please bring your musical instrument to comfort me." As the request was from his benefactor, Delille was unlikely to refuse.

The ruse worked perfectly. Ten minutes after the letter arrived, I was out the door and in search of Uncle Léon's home on Rue Lafitte. When I found it, the edifice was no less imposing than I had expected. I sounded the clapper and tried to quell my nervous fidgeting. The first face to appear was a servant boy's; a dainty pinched face whose squinty eyes opened wide when I said "Monsieur Saint-Germain expects me. I am his nephew."

"You need no proof but your face," said Léon, who had been standing out of my view behind the door.

He was a handsome man, tall and distinctive in dress, with thick hair the color of dark wheat. Léon was perhaps twenty years older than I, and I was flattered to think that he saw a resemblance. Inside, the marble foyer gave further proof of his successful investments in what my father called "some kind of banking ventures."

After an exchange of pleasantries about Paris and my family in Saint-Rémy, I suddenly abandoned my manners and bluntly asked if he could arrange another position.

"Perhaps," he said slowly, "but only if you tell me truthfully of your reason for leaving Delille."

I described the situation, altering it slightly. "If you could arrange another position, I assure you I'll never again risk bringing shame to the family name."

Uneasily I awaited his response; expecting to be chastised. But after what seemed an endless silence, he broke into a sly laugh and said, "You seem like no son of my straitlaced brother." Of all unimagined twists! He was delighted by my story, while I had tormented myself with contrition.

Léon assured me I would be freed of my obligations to old Delille and that he would secure another apprenticeship.

"I shall inform him I have need of you as aide during my illness," he grinned, as though enjoying the deception.

The same arrogant little groom, who had opened the door for me and whose shoulders came only to my belt clasp, led me to my quarters. And what fine quarters they were: a merciful contrast to Monsieur Delille's musty roomlet. The chambers were large and airy, with an armoire of carved oak large enough to contain seven times my wardrobe, a tapestry-upholstered chair with arms fashioned after the clawed paws of a mythical beast, and a canopied bed covered with a spread of fabric which must have taken five weavers a year of blinding labor to produce.

That afternoon, while Uncle Léon attended to his business affairs, I happily waited in my room, alone and idle. In dreamy abstraction I gazed out the window, which gave onto an herb garden, bright and aromatic in the spring breeze. In this felicitous yet unfamiliar place, with the scent of crushed mint wafting from the garden, I was snared by the first tentative words of a poem.

Barely pausing to adjust the strings, I positioned my lute and strummed a few notes, prompted by an emerging mood. The song grew slowly, with hesitant words and rearranging of notes, until my ears told me they were true. At first, I sang of Françoise, but the woman soon ceased to be she and the lady of the poem assumed another visage: the eyes of which I sang no longer glinted with a craving for danger but were trusting eyes, and tranquil; and though this lady was also wedded to a man for whom she had no love, it was I who courted her away from fidelity. I sang of what might have been, transforming the past into a ballad false to memory but true to imagination.

I had just begun the final line of music and was searching for the unresolved chord when Léon called from beyond my door. I promptly set aside the lute and my notations, smoothed my rumpled coat and followed him to the end of a long hallway. We entered a library, its walls solidly lined with richly bound volumes. As I breathed in the mingled smells of leather and wood smoke from the carved marble fireplace, I felt simultaneously awed by and yet worthy of the atmosphere of prosperity in which I found myself.

"Be seated, Nephew," he said, pointing to a chair near the fire. "Now, besides the distraction of Delille's wife, did you find the printing trade to your liking?"

"No," I answered readily, "it was a tiresome, dirty business and while not without some interest, uninspiring."

Léon's tone turned condescending. "So, you seek an apprenticeship which inspires you. And what might that be?"

"I find that my muse prefers handsome quarters to a garret and I am loathe to wake up each morning stained with the last day's grime. I'd rather do a job which demands more of my brain than of my shoulders."

"Handsome quarters you'll not get, once you've left my home. Your room is customarily reserved for visiting noblemen. Several dukes and a prince have slept in that same bed."

"Forgive me, Uncle, I did not mean to be presumptuous."

"Perhaps it is a failing we share, Nephew, but you state your demands too baldly. Yet I do have something in mind, for I could possibly have a friend arrange an appointment in the court. Of course, your lodgings will be modest, but your days and nights will be spent in the milieu you desire. As Delille may have mentioned, I am of no small influence among those in courtly circles."

I accepted his offer calmly, while under my breath I whispered a tremulous prayer of thanksgiving to the Virgin.

"As you are my kindred, your position will be recompense to me for favors owed. The chains of debt and repayment in Paris are unending, and so I will exact a fee from you. If you accept, you shall be my own discreet agent within the walls."

I was to report to Uncle Léon twice each fortnight. His business was moneylending, his clients those highly placed in court or the relatives thereof. The interest he received was, strictly speaking, usurious. But those who sought his services gladly paid the exorbitant interest in order to use his funds. Since the rates he charged were illegal though not uncommon, if one of his clients could not pay there was no legal recourse. Thus I would keep Léon informed of those who were in or out of favor, since the latter were most likely to cause him an irretrievable loss.

"The price seems small."

"Nothing to give your conscience unrest. Your ears will be mine, as regards court matters."

I thanked him in a voice so subdued it was barely audible. Uncle Léon regarded me curiously. "You do not seem surprised by this turn of events. Your complacency puzzles me."

I offered no explanation. I had not foreseen this boon, yet I had had a vague premonition that the city of Paris would not be close-handed with me.

Before he dismissed me, Uncle Léon outlined a program. I would need to be tutored in manners and fitted out with new clothes. Of more importance, I would have to be informed of the partisan divisions within court. "And then," he added, "before your appointment begins, you shall travel as my emissary to deliver a parcel in Carcassonne. Consider the journey as a stage in your training."

I would not be far from my family or from Montpellier! "I would like to visit my family and a close friend who is presently studying medicine near Carcassonne," I began.

"Of course you may. Another few days will not matter. I shall arrange for your duties to begin in six weeks, but first we shall devote the coming week to your wardrobe and *maintien*. You must apply and make keen your manners, then travel as a nobleman." He paused a moment, considered my appearance and said, "We do have a job laid out for us. We'll have to pare away the unpleasant crust of both student life and printer's apprentice."

No doubt he referred to superficial habits. Uncle Léon was inclined, on occasion, to state matters baldly.

On the third day, he called me back to his library.

"Tell me, Alain," he began, "what are your sentiments on the subject of, shall we say, divergent religious sects?"

I ventured an evasive reply. "While I was a student, I listened to stories of abuses which led to the rise of renegade religious groups, stories of immorality and greed, stories of priests who cohabit with nuns in secret underground passageways and of bishops who sell dispensations for gold. And yet," I added, "in Saint-Rémy the Churchmen were kind and sincere; in Avignon I found them learned and devout."

I mentioned, too, the number of forbidden printed tracts condemning the Church which were circulated in my school, the students who stood in clusters and whispered over them.

"I know not what to believe," I said finally. "You place me in an awkward position, Uncle; you must have an interest either in the old Church or in the new movement, although I cannot discern which."

"I attend Mass, I receive Holy Communion...because it is politic to do so."

"Then your piety is only affectation!"

"You may conclude so, if you wish. We will not discuss it further today. Your task is to gather information for me impartially, as though I am a devout Churchman and also an oppositionist. Overlook no rumor. Our King shifts his policies, thus does the court, and so must I."

So began my lesson in polity and court intrigue. Uncle Léon explained it was doubtful whether King François would venture far from the Church, for he had little to gain. Unlike his contemporary Henry of England, François had papal consent to appoint bishops and abbots, which meant payment and power were already in his own hands. But Uncle Léon saw no end to the Protestant movement, so strong was its momentum and so varied its adherents. "Moreover," he said, "who knows which position the young Dauphin will adopt once he is King?"

"But that is years away—he's only a boy," I said, wondering how many rulers my uncle intended to outlive.

"Years, perhaps, many or few. I am always packed and ready for change and when it occurs I need alter my life but slightly; a realignment of gesture and phrase, a few coins spread in the right direction, and a new future is secured."

"Until the next upheaval."

"I find this no encumbrance to living fully. It stimulates me on to a lively old age."

The groom reappeared to refresh our wine cups. Intentionally, no doubt, he spilled a few drops on my wrinkled doublet, and, thinking his apology insincere, I glowered at him until he departed.

With our privacy restored, Uncle Léon told me of the King's taste for lavish spending. With a treasury near bankruptcy, François had sworn to limit his indulgences, yet rumors spread that another campaign might be advanced into Italy for the fattening of French coffers and the enhancement of the King's magnificence.

I understood that I was to make rumors my business. The names and various family connections swam in my head. Léon assured me they would soon become clear, but the day left me tired and perplexed. I was to disregard no one, for power is held often in unlikely hands, by those prominent in the bedchamber as well as in the chamber of council.

He urged me to observe the friendships and enmities of the family de Guise, who he explained were the lords of the duchy of Lorraine. "You will see them often in court," he advised. "Learn to read their manner as though you were following a map, for in their direction may lie the future of France and the fate of the line of the Valois.

"At first, you will be able only to report details I

already know. On the basis of these early reports, I will be in a position to appraise your perception and judgment. Soon you shall outdistance my own ready information; then your value will be potentially immeasurable, for I am here and you will be within the walls."

At the close of my last lesson he handed me a purse containing a hundred crowns, and I was told a servant would escort me.

"Do not regard him as a comrade," said my uncle, "for he is your inferior, and when you enter royal service, you are to retain a nobleman's air. The dignity of your position demands this." I thought of his arrogant little groom. "Always remember," he said finally, "you too have been served."

I departed early the following morning while the river's mist hovered about the twin towers of Notre Dame, clad in a fine new suit of bottle-green velvet trimmed with black braid and brass buttons. I rode a restive gray mare who became more manageable once we had turned onto country roads, and at my side was a tired old servant named Jacques, sleepily mounted on a gelded roan.

The first day I was miserable with this unnecessary human baggage; for one thing, it was my natural tendency to converse but as I had been instructed by Uncle Léon to avoid familiarity, therefore Jacques and I rode in a silence broken only by hoofbeats and bird song. After our stop at a roadhouse near Montargis, I came to accept my time-withered escort, even to appreciate his gentle husbandry of the horses and his fastidious attendance to my garments. With his wrinkled hand and a brush he could restore luster to a horse's coat or to a dusty riding cloak.

On the twelfth day we entered the city of Montpellier and made our lodgings in a hostelry adjacent to the college. It was an inn renowned for fairly clean linen and promised a nightly fare of delectable and varied stew. I left Jacques at the inn with instructions to unpack my parcels; meanwhile, I set out for the college of medicine in hope that once I had arrived, someone would direct me to Michel de Nostredame.

Beyond a densely forbidding door with a pair of heavy iron pulls, the bustle of Montpellier subsided and I found myself standing in a damp and musty hallway. From a nearby room a droning professorial voice held forth on the subject of fractures. My eyes, now accustomed to the muted light, looked up the dim corridor and counted a dozen lecture halls. I was dejected. The trip had been tiring, but throughout I had bolstered my spirits by anticipating the moment when I would again see Michel. In my naïveté, I had failed to consider the problem of locating him.

The droning voice ceased and in a great rustle of black robes, students spilled through the doorway, into the hall where I waited. I searched their preoccupied faces for the familiar one—or would it be? Only a year had passed, but I had changed from a round-cheeked student in rumpled clothes and an unpredictable slit of a shy smile to a soon-to-become royal attendant in velvet livery with a bold, ready countenance and a dark blond beard now grown thick, though I kept it in careful trim.

The youths with their dark robes and full unkempt beards looked like a unified mass of wool and whiskers as they walked down the passageway. Thinking that surely Michel had distinguished himself as a student (soon he would receive his physician's license), I supposed I had only to ask in order to be directed to him. And indeed, events soon proved me correct.

A professor walked past, cutting a swath through the crowd of students. To catch his attention, I spoke boldly. Following my uncle's advice, I assumed a nobleman's air and could sense by the professor's deference that he thought me to be of high birth.

"I seek a student named Michel de Nostredame, great-grandson of the physician to King René."

His glance lingered on my brass collar button. "I was not aware of young Michel's heritage, sir," the doctor remarked, "but if you attend my next lecture, you will find him there for he never misses a word. Diligence does him credit and compensates for his unorthodox medical notions."

He peered at me with some wariness. "May I inquire after your interest?"

"I am a relative visiting Montpellier on court matters," I lied. The doctor said hastily, "I did not intend to disparage Michel de Nostredame, for he is a remarkable student. A bit rebellious now, but when he embarks upon his own practice I trust he will discover that traditional methods are best; they are most comforting to the patient and most comfortable for the physician." He caressed the large stone of his gleaming ruby ring and said, "My next lecture begins at the eleventh hour."

And at the eleventh hour, Michel appeared. He had a tangled dark beard and in most respects was indistinguishable from the others; indeed, it was not Michel whom I recognized, but the imprint of his father's stern visage. He identified me at once, though. I flattered myself to think news had reached him of a smart courtier who sought his audience. I held my chin aloft as he approached, aware of my distinctive presence amidst slovenly students and portly red-robed professors.

"Welcome to Montpellier, Alain," he said dryly. "Our modest town will seem an uneventful place after Paris." He scrutinized my costume. "I see you are prosperous, too; a printer's apprentice must be well-paid."

I felt like a peacock in a convent, suddenly desirous of plainer clothes and Michel's understanding. I mumbled an apology for my discordant dress and explained that I was no longer apprentice to a printer, but was soon to begin duties in King François's court, and that my Uncle Léon had made the arrangements.

"My congratulations," said Michel, with such thinly concealed scorn that I was galled into protest: "You once spoke about the worth of our friendship. Do superficial details matter so greatly?" I asked.

Michel smiled reluctantly, as though he was little practiced in pleasure, then he said, "Well, my dear poet, you force me to admit I am pleased to see you. We were always as far apart in some ways as the midheaven and nadir."

"As you once said, I was born of the sun and you of Saturn. How goes it, with your study of the stars?"

"I've not entirely forgotten what I learned in Avignon—no thanks to your specious scheme. In practice, I spend three-quarters of my time studying medicine, one-eighth on astral studies, by which time I am exhausted and can't wait for my portion of sleep."

"No wonder you appear so grim; you've no time left for love."

"Or for any other vice," he said curtly, and reminded me that the anatomy lecture was soon to begin. He asked if I cared to attend, assuring me the professor would not object. We thus concluded our conversation on a strained note and followed the other students into the lecture hall, taking two remaining bench seats toward the rear. An anatomical diagram rested on a tripod before the class in the revered space where a moment later the professor would be applauded on entry with cries of *"Vivat!"*

For a tedious hour the eminent doctor shuffled his notes and tapped out examples on the chart with a long black pointer. I tried to pay attention out of courtesy but the lines denoting musculature and viscera were a confused tangle to my untrained eye. I confessed this to Michel after the lecture (to account for my uncontrollable yawning) while we strolled toward the Grey Swan for our midday meal.

"An anatomical rendering is sadly inadequate compared to real work with a cadaver," he said, telling me that during the last year, when he was still a new student, he had been quite outspoken on the matter of dissection, but that he wasted his voice. "The doctors are blind as worms," he said. "They teach us to debate a fine point as though this was the goal of education. I am here to learn the healers' art and sometimes I think Montpellier is nothing but an impediment. But no matter, this exercise in irrelevance will soon end."

I took the devil's defense and suggested that his understanding could not be hindered by studying anatomy and the signs of illness.

"Formulas and rules. Greater vision is needed in the

art of healing to see where the rules of medicine and symbols either meet or diverge."

We walked toward the River Lez. The autumn sun filtered through the trees, casting dappled shadows on our path.

"This is not the most direct route to my favorite hostelry," said Michel, holding his hand palm upward as if to gather the shadow imprint of the leaves above us, "but I favor the autumn months when every color of nature seems in a state of transformation. The view is best from the river's edge, and I come here often to untangle my thoughts."

To me it was not especially interesting, yet I could appreciate how the gently flowing current and the vista of the city behind us might indeed soothe the over-wrought mind of a medical student whose conflicting thoughts required two different notebooks.

We descended a stone stairway to what would have been, in springtime, a grassy bank. Now it was dry, prickly to sit on. But I imagined it greened over, with a girl in arm's reach and a flagon of wine cooling nearby in the reeds. The still-warm sun and lack of shade prompted Michel to remove his heavy outer robe. Over the thinner woolen garment beneath, I saw a largish cloth pouch hanging from a belt at his hip. He saw me looking curiously upon it and said, "Oh, I meant to show you my new treasure. It is an astrolabe—have you ever seen one?"

I admitted I had not. I knew only that such instruments were used by seamen, and that they had some astrological application as well.

Michel pulled a metal disk from the pouch, and on its face was another inlaid disk, with a single dia-metrical rule or indicator intersecting the two circles. He turned it over and on the back was a map of the constellations.

"These pointers show the positions of the stars, rel-ative to one another and in relation to the sun. With this table I can quickly see the planetary aspects on any given day. And by rotating this arm or *rete* I can read from this line of coincidence the time of day."

I held it, turned it around and nodded approvingly, though the astrolabe offered me no such information. Perhaps it took many lessons to manipulate it correctly. It was a handsome device, though, with a clever fretwork design around its perimeter.

"Now that you have seen my meditation place and my new trinket, I will lead you to the famous Grey Swan, as promised."

Once inside the packed inn, redolent with the aroma of spices and savory broth, we seated ourselves at a crowded wooden table, its surface scarred by decades of platters and carving knives. Michel signaled to the innkeeper, who soon placed steaming bowls of fish chowder before us.

"Are you still penning your poetry?" Michel asked me between mouthfuls.

"Not as often as I'd hoped, but I am satisfied with a few verses. Here, I have copied one from my journal for you, though perhaps it is a misnomer to call it a 'journal' since I do not write in it daily. The material in it is nonetheless culled from events and circumstances that could surely be reconstructed by the calendar."

I took a slim roll of parchment from my doublet; on it I had copied the love poem transfigured from my memory of Françoise Delille. As Michel unrolled the page and read the quatrains, I was confident of his approval and continued to dip into my savory soup.

"However eloquent, I will not commend you for glorifying illicit love," he said shortly.

I was startled at first and momentarily distressed, but then I realized that this black-robed young man had never been in Paris. He was sheltered from the delight and anguish of what, to me, comprised the real world; because he had never loved a woman, on him even the most exquisitely chaste love poem would be lost.

"I grant you a point there," I said lightly. I could afford to be pliant for I was convinced of the vitality of my work and felt no need to defend it. Yet his respect was important to me. I turned to a page in my journal and read him another verse, one which I'd composed specifically for the occasion of our reunion. It had been

inspired by Michel's purity of character, and while I
believed it to be less well-crafted, it was to the point:

> The heart untouched is nearest God
> > When the gift of love is bestowed at last
> As in your eyes I see mirrored my gaze
> > Alone in His sight is our love blessed.

"Needs a bit of polish, but the sentiment shines
through," said Michel with a twinkle. "I think you are
not so reprobate as you like to appear. But you should
be concerned for your eternal soul and not let shadows
become your reality."

"This is truly a remarkable chowder," I said uneasily, taking his words to heart. Faith had become a matter of defense to me; I prayed mainly when obstacles
arose and I attended Mass frequently enough to keep
the saints' power on my side. But what of Michel? What
was his faith? I broached the subject distantly and asked,
"What do you think of Luther and his followers? Are
the Reformers merely indulging in theological peevish-
ness or is there just cause for condemning the Roman
Church?"

"The criticism is justifiable," he replied, "but the
Church has endured over a thousand years, and she
will endure a thousand more."

"You speak with such certainty," I remarked, then
spliced on the opinion of Uncle Léon: "I personally think
the Church may be supplanted by a new order within
our lifetime."

It occurred to me that Michel may have been so out-
spokenly loyal to the Church and convinced of its con-
tinuance as a safeguard for himself. Did he speak in a
publicly pious voice because he feared to be known as
a Jew, or to mask his interest in other studies?

"Tell me of your own faith," I asked. "You once said
something to the effect that the study of the stars was
more beneficial than a thousand hours before the altar."

"I spoke from ignorance then," Michel explained. "The
longer I study, the clearer it becomes that the Roman
Church is catholic or universal because it has absorbed
the teachings of the Hebrews, the Greeks and many

secret sects of ancient times." He lowered his voice and continued, "I have been studying an Egyptian treatise in which the ancient god Osiris dies and is resurrected in early spring, like the Christ. This does not undermine my faith, but only strengthens it, for my faith is not in gods but in symbols represented by them, and by these tokens we climb closer to our God. I believe in the Church, in her calendar of rites and saints. Such richness satisfies the souls of most men, but here is where I differ and where I must exercise caution when I speak, for the Church is to me as a childhood home which I must leave and venture forth to reach my own maturity of spirit."

With my curiosity satisfied to know that beneath it all Michel was a Christian (and to avoid entering a theological discussion for which I was ill-prepared) I returned to a more mundane topic.

"As a connoisseur of Montpellier cuisine, how can you forswear this innkeeper's other dishes?" Lenten season was to begin the following day.

"It may surprise you to know that I regularly fast; not only on days prescribed by the Church, but for another reason. I find that it liberates me from the distractions of mealtime and enables me to attain greater concentration."

I mentioned that my work would also benefit by improved concentration.

"What need have you of concentration? You've chosen, with enthusiasm, a continually distracting life in court."

"Yes, but the lives I shall observe, the spectrum of courtiers and ladies, will fill my journals and provide inspiration for my poems."

"My concentration would not suit you, for I can only command it on serious occasions. But tell me, Alain, what *will* your new court duties entail?"

I told him that I would be assistant to the princes' tutor and added that I had agreed to keep my Uncle Léon informed about circumstances within the court. "I'm afraid that the nursery is a poor place to gather information," I said, somewhat embarrassed about my actual position.

"No doubt you will have much of interest to tell your uncle, in time," Michel ventured. "I have a few speculations of my own. Some are based on the rumors that find their way to us here in Montpellier; for example, I hear that the Duke of Bourbon may attempt to seize Provence."

"It is possible," I confirmed. "Rumors trade cheaply and far."

"But sometimes I have dreams...and they have nothing to do with rumors I have heard. My visions appear with a great feeling of certainty, though the meaning remains unclear. I often write them in my notebooks, and it makes for strange reading."

"Sometimes my verses make for strange reading, too," I said.

"Perhaps you have not found your subject," Michel suggested. "You are concerned now with the intimate portrait, with *amour*—but in your new life you will be surrounded with talk of military campaigns and the elements of power. Perhaps you should widen your sites," he said, leaning forward on the plank seat with a new glimmer of excitement in his eyes. "Perhaps you could write an epic poem of France—a work of real consequence!"

But I was not inspired, and only many years later did I realize that he took his own advice to heart. Or maybe he had a premonition of a sweeping work to come, yet remained unclear of its authorship. In any case, our time together in Montpellier was brief, but as I look back on it now, our words revealed directions in which we each would travel. And so we parted after that meal, and I said, "Next time we meet, you will be dressed in the four-pointed hat and will be wearing your physician's ring." To this, Michel parried: "And you, my friend, will be wearing a different shade of velvet."

My return to Paris was blighted by foul weather. Riding into heavy rains on a barren stretch of road my horse lost a shoe in the muck. If traveling alone I would have been forced to dismount and slosh along on foot for many miles to the next village, but as Jacques was with me, I simply shared his roan and the incident caused no delay but the hour required to shoe my mare at a village smith.

The storm clouds had moved south by the time we arrived at my uncle's home, and I arose the next day ready for my new role. With care, I chose a brown velvet tunic and accepted Léon's offer of a carriage ride to Les Tournelles. He assured me I was expected.

No doubt great favors were owed my uncle, for my comrades in attendance were all of noble birth, and the only flawed moment of the first day came when one of them asked how a nobody like myself came into such a choice position. The mention of Léon Saint-Germain won me immediate apology and that night a flask of cognac appeared anonymously in my room.

The young Dauphin was only six years old, but as I watched him playing in the nursery I thought: Someday this runny-nosed child will be King and here I am, amidst assorted playthings and nurses, tending to his needs. I judged that my uncle would want me to become indispensable, and so I did. I charmed the nannies and soon came to be regarded by Queen Claude as the most conscientious of attendants. Proudly I told Uncle Léon this at our next meeting.

"Because she is Queen you ascribe power to her, but have you noticed how rarely the King is with her?" he asked irritably.

"I thought he was busy with his military advisers. There is the trouble over Provence."

"Where are you hiding your ears? The King is devoted to his mistress, Madame de Chateaubriant, and before her there was another. Get yourself in *her* good graces; forget the nannies and Queen Claude."

"But what of the royal children? Surely I should cultivate the Dauphin's affection above all else."

"In part, but if he succeeds to the throne while in his minority, Queen Claude will be regent and will be controlled by François's counselors. You would be wise to ingratiate yourself to them. And if the Dauphin were to die, Henri, Duc d'Orleans would inherit the throne, so do not neglect him either."

* * *

Following my uncle's advice, I extended my attentions to both children, and in application of this prudence, the pattern of my days became more complex. I found my eyes darting about constantly to see who passed through the hallways; some nights my dreams bristled with fragments of conversation I had cadged during the day.

Fostering the affections of both the Dauphin and young Henri was no chore, for the children were amiable. The Dauphin had inherited the King's easy manner and his love of entertainment, while Henri was more quiet but a contented child who doted on his mother. I found myself favoring him, though he was twice removed from the throne. During that year, when a third prince was born, I decided to limit my attention to the two eldest; later, my instincts proved correct.

After I had been in court for only a few months, an incident occurred which outraged all of France, one whose effects would be felt for many years.

The Duke of Bourbon attempted to seize Provence, but the campaign failed and his troops were driven away by François's army. In the glow of victory, and in retaliation against the Emperor Charles of Spain, who had supported the duke's campaign, François led his army into Milan but the venture proved tragic. In the battle at Pavia, not only did France suffer a shameful defeat, but in a monstrous turn of events the King himself was captured and taken to prison in Madrid.

Two years of futile negotiations followed. Of prime importance was the release of the sovereign, who was not only captive but at one point was near death from illness and exhaustion.

During those years, the court was neither gay nor bristling with information to relay to my uncle. All factions were unified in their concern for the King's return, and in his absence the Queen Mother Louise ruled with astringency; she was a lady who couldn't be charmed. But I was young, I reminded myself, and when this gloomy period had passed and a treaty was at last ratified, the court would return to its previous splendor.

In the long, hot months when Paris sweltered, the

residents of Les Tournelles sought refuge in the chateau at Blois where fresh air blew across open fields of blossoms and passed coolly over the Loire to perfume and refresh us. As attendant to the children, I was included in the entourage and it was at Blois that I came to understand François's passion for architecture. In the sculpted stonework of the country chateau were a thousand details to savor. The dominant theme repeated throughout the summer palace, appearing on mantels and in cornices, was the salamander: the King's own device. Its presence offered reassurance, for the salamander is believed to rise from flames unscathed, and so, we prayed, would he.

The times were tense, waiting for emergence, and other dreadful news was borne to the country where we carried on a dispirited routine. A plague had descended on the south of France.

I received a letter from Michel late in that year, 1525. In it, he assured me that my family and his had been spared, and that the pestilence had gone from Saint-Rémy. Judging by the date he had inscribed at the top of the letter, May 13, I knew many months had passed in the composing of it, and several months more before it was delivered into my hands the following March. At first, I wondered that he had chosen me for his unburdening. But were I faced with such terrible sights and the chance of never again seeing family or friends, perhaps I too would wish to tell another of it. Now, only a fragment of the letter remains:

My Dear Alain,

I write to assure you that Saint-Rémy has had little incidence of the pestilence. The sickness there has run its course and your family and mine remain in good health.

How often I have thought of you and of our visit in Montpellier, for shortly thereafter I departed the college without completing my final studies when I heard that *le charbon* had stricken the cities of Provence and Languedoc, and that many physicians had fled to protect themselves, leaving the inhabitants helpless.

In the first town where I offered my services, Béziers, I was deceived by the apparent mildness of the pestilence. Though when I resumed my journey, I witnessed the disease in its full horror and dread.

When Michel entered the city gates of Béziers, no sign of the pestilence was evident. People strolled the streets, seemingly concerned only with the day's price of almonds, olive oil or other produce. The shutters of shop fronts were open and tradesmen busied themselves pleasing customers. Michel paused before a barber's stall where the barber was removing a towel from a ruddy-faced client. Michel recalled that he had intended to have a haircut before leaving Montpellier; he indicated to the barber that he wished to be next. A small dog, mascot of the shop, sniffed at Michel's boot.

"Your business thrives," Michel observed, removing his hat. By its distinctive shape, the barber knew this customer was a physician; by the unfamiliarity of Michel's face, he knew that the man he was about to groom was no resident of Béziers.

"You would be a visiting doctor from Montpellier, I'll wager." He sharpened his razor and remarked, "I see no need for extra medics in Béziers. Between me and the doctors, we keep our people fit. Of course, there's a kind of simple pox going about lately, but those who get it are up and around within a day or two."

Michel sighed. His errand of mercy, undertaken with burning purpose, seemed unnecessary. "I shall need lodging for the night, at least. Could you recommend an inn?"

"Since you are newly arrived, I'll cut your hair, trim the beard and put you up in my spare room, all for a modest charge."

The barber had correctly gauged the disease; in Béziers it was mild, though widespread. Michel found he could be of assistance to the harried local doctors, though, and thus he administered to a few patients. Standard medications sufficed in every case; the pustules, while causing discomfort, quickly subsided, and in only one of Michel's patients did they even require lancing.

Michel's youth caused the older doctors to regard him as a junior handyman. He was sent to apply a splint to a broken arm, he was asked to carry orders to the apothecary, and only once did he rankle when a resident physician told him to cauterize a patient who suffered from a gunshot wound. Michel refused, saying his method was to treat it with soothing dressings; if the doctor wished to cauterize the patient, he could do so himself.

At the end of his month's stay in Béziers, Michel became restless. He paid the balance owed for his lodging, mentioning to the barber that he intended to take his mule and ride southwest to Narbonne where there might be greater need of his services.

"We have closed the gates to those who come from that city," said the barber. "They are dying like flies in Narbonne; I'd not go there, if I were you."

Michel hardly knew what to expect when he arrived at the walled city, for Béziers had shown him the ravage of disease only in miniature. Soon he would see, beside the pustules or buboes, severe cases accompanied by diarrhea, and lungs so filled with fluid that each cough would sound like a death rattle until, at last, a final convulsion would prove it so.

Yet in his ignorance, Michel was confident. He would strive to ease their suffering; for his part, he was well-fed, rested, strong, and he entertained no thought that he might also succumb. But after the day's ride he faced a sight that shattered his confidence; there a festering death cart conveying a pile of corpses to the pit graves outside the walled city rumbled past. Limp bodies jostled about as one of the cart wheels struck a stone in the roadway. Arms and legs askew, four corpses tumbled over the side and landed in a foul tangle before him.

Shaken by this omen, he entered Narbonne, his hat and robe revealing that he was a student of medicine. Inside the gate, he asked a stranger where lodgings might be found.

"A doctor," sneered the man, taking sight of the robe beneath Michel's traveling cloak. "Can you exorcise de-

mons from the body? Do you change a man's destiny?"
He clutched at Michel's cloak, his mouth a gaping hole
picked with broken teeth. Michel shoved the man aside
and evaded his grasp, but the accusing voice pursued
Michel as he walked fearfully up the street. He tried
to make sense of the man's distressed words, thinking
him perhaps a follower of Luther, or someone who
blamed another physician for the loss of a brother, wife
or child.

From an open doorway the head of a younger man
appeared; he called for help. Michel nodded in assent,
and as he stooped to enter the low doorway he recognized the symptoms immediately: The woman lay on a
linen sheet, livid red sores protruding from her pale
skin. As Michel raised the sheet and inspected the swollen glands, she stared at him with wide, terrified eyes,
for the disease was in a stage of advancement which
yielded full consciousness.

Her husband knelt at the bedside, rosary clasped in
his hands. "You shall be made well," he whispered.
Although the husband's certainty rendered Michel tem-
porarily immobile, his eyes ranged analytically over
the woman's body. He could lance her sores, but unless
he could devise another treatment for her he feared that
the husband's prayers might be her best hope.

Then a clarity of mind came upon Michel and he
noticed the features of the woman's face; her damp hair-
line, the brown limp hair pushed from her brow and
the gentle curve of her chin were reminiscent of a pale
lunar orb. So compelling was the image that he asked
the young husband if his wife would celebrate her birth-
day in the following month.

"Yes, and if God wills her to live, she will be twenty."

Michel's question assumed uncannily accurate information, but the man was so distraught that he did
not think it odd for this physician to speculate as to her
month of birth. Child of the moon and twenty. That
placed her birth two years later than Michel's. Knowing
the position of her sun, and from memory recalling the
exact positions of the slower moving planets, Saturn
and Jupiter, in his own horoscope, to this he added the
rapidly moving Mercury, Mars and Venus, making hasty

calculations in his mind to reconstruct her natal con-
figuration. With a leap from the star-patterns in his
memory, he concluded that a concoction of two herbs
would aid her. He used no time-proven medical axioms
for guidance, nor had he accurate mathematical calculations on which to base his procedure, but as he
lanced and cleared the abscesses he read her body like
the most lucid of diagrams.

Michel handed the bloody strips of linen to the husband, who threw them into the spitting hearth where
flames soon turned cloth to ash. "I must find an apothecary," Michel said.

"One remains. His shop is seventh on the row."

"Where may I lodge? I cannot aid others for long if
I do not provide some food and rest for myself." Because
of his exhaustion, Michel's words were harsh.

"You will pass a hostelry on the way to the apothecary," said the man, "but first, I beg you, return to me
with the medicine you have promised." With a despair-
ing look, the husband watched the departure of the
physician he had prayed for, the physician who left
behind a patient in greater agony than before his arrival.

Michel returned in early evening; by candlelight in
the darkened room he tipped a cup to the woman's
cracked lips. Time and again he forced her to drink
until, when she was unable to drink more, he left the
half-filled jar to be spooned to her throughout the night.

At the inn, he fell upon his bed after swallowing a
few bites of bread and a small portion of broth, exhausted from the day's ordeal. He craved sleep yet fought
it, for he had tended to only one patient while hundreds
needed his help; their moans and cries pursued him
even after he let go of wakefulness and fell into a deep
sleep.

That night Michel dreamed he possessed a wonderful
hound, a fine and loyal creature of clear eye and glossy
coat. But one morning as he went to feed it, he saw
with horror that the sleek body had turned to a transparent and shimmering substance. Though the dog yet
lived, it was not aware of his presence, and Michel knew

with the familiar chill of certainty that this unearthly state was a precursor of death.

Michel woke from the dream soaked in sweat to find the sun had long since risen over the town. Through the glazed window he saw the half-timbered buildings of Narbonne and remembered the immensity of his task: They waited for *him,* dozens of victims within a few steps of his inn, hundreds all told, for of the few doctors left, almost all had barricaded themselves in their homes and refused to touch any victim stricken by the pestilence.

Michel hurriedly ate a bowl of gruel and drank a mug of hot water, then he returned to the house of his patient. After his dream of the night before, he expected to find the boils swollen with poison, the patient unconscious and on the rim of death. But when the husband greeted Michel at the door, his face was haggard yet beaming, for during the night the inflamed abscesses had receded, and after much feverish tossing and profuse perspiration, the woman had slept peacefully until morning, when she had awakened suddenly and requested food.

"She will live," the husband said with surety, as if his belief had made it so. Gazing in astonishment at her now, while recalling her condition of the previous day, Michel had to agree that the crisis was past. Cautiously he reminded the elated husband that it would be weeks before his wife would be pronounced as fully recovered.

As he walked away from the home, he shook his head in amazement and thanksgiving, for the direful dream was only an expression of his fears and was not prophetic of death—or so it seemed to Michel that day.

Michel treated his next several patients with equal success. No longer did he even inquire as to the patient's nativity, for his intuition became infallible in such matters, and correspondingly he became confident of his ability to effect a cure in even the most extreme cases. But his success aroused the jealousy of the few physicians who had not abandoned their patients and who now faced the indignity of having them cured by this itinerant doctor. They could not deny Michel's efficacy, yet they had recourse to another defense: condemnation of Michel's unorthodox practices.

As Michel worked, he noticed countless variations in the symptoms of the same disease; through his observations and experiments he found the correlation between healing herbs and planetary influence of increasing interest. Noticing his fascination, the apothecary who had first aided him in making his decoctions discreetly introduced Michel to a frail old man who resided in a tiny room behind a woolen shop: his name was Simon LeCler, a nominally Christian Jew.

In Simon's windowless room, which had the advantage of not being visible from the street, Michel was to study the esoteric teachings of the Cabala. On his first visit to Simon's, he saw on the walls of this secret academy a painted scroll, yellowed with age, portraying the Tree of Life; the tree which Jean de Saint-Rémy had described to him many years before. Within his heart he still carried his grandfather's secret teachings, almost forgotten, but there in the tiny room behind the woolen shop he saw again the mysterious tree depicted on parchment, twelve sacred branches with the mystic letters of creation at the terminus of each limb.

The first night Michel arrived shortly after sunset. A young man who introduced himself as Simon LeCler's son handed him a small rush mat. Legs folded beneath him, Michel took his place along with four other men who sat on the bare floor. The table on which Simon stacked his sections of wool was pushed to a far corner. Against the wall, the tailor sat on a rush mat, eyes closed. After a long silence he spoke:

"En Soph fills and encloses the universe. As He is boundless, the mind cannot contain Him. From His being, the ten Sephiroth emanate like rays from the sun. The visible is a measure of the invisible; it proceeds by analogy from the known to the unknown. Each fragment of nature, each part of the human body, corresponds to a portion of the unseen universe. It is to see more clearly this Oneness that we are gathered here tonight."

Afterward Michel sat stilly to preserve the precious awe in which he was engulfed as he sat on his rush mat, for in only a few words LeCler had explained the encompassing order that Michel had discovered independently through his healing. He was not alone, nor was he mad; others had seen what he had, and their vision was recorded long before his birth. He smiled to think that each day in his life was only a process of rediscovery, rediscovery of that which had been lost to the memory of mankind.

Each night when he left his last patient, Michel went to study at the side of Simon LeCler; there for a few hours the suffering he had witnessed during the day was forgotten. But his apprenticeship would only last a few weeks before threats forced Michel to return to the road. It happened thus...

One day while Michel was spooning a pungent decoction of bay and poppy seed into the thin lips of an elderly woman, a corpulent man in red robes entered the patient's home. He stood quietly, assessing Michel's procedures.

"You there," he said, "by what license do you practice medicine?"

"As I have been tending your own neglected patients, it may relieve your conscience to know that I studied medicine at Montpellier."

"I am relieved to know you did not learn your skills beneath a hedge," he said, snatching the jar from Michel's hand and sniffing its contents. "I understand you do not administer geysers nor do you examine the patient's urine before prescribing these concoctions."

"I find little merit in listening to the pulse, nor in judging by paltry piss," Michel replied.

The doctor reddened to the crimson of his mantle, then he turned angrily and stalked from the room, pausing in the doorway to add with a cruel smile, "I speak for all physicians in Narbonne. Your success is due either to irresponsible good chance or to witchcraft. For the second you could burn. There are now a dozen physicians ready to tend those suffering from the pestilence; therefore your services are no longer needed. Do not delay in leaving or we shall make it public that you are a practitioner of the black arts."

That night when Michel walked toward Simon Le-Cler's room, a hooded man followed him closely. With defiant pleasure, Michel led him on a labyrinthine walk, making several detours through winding alleyways and once strolling in a full circle around a long block of buildings. When he returned to his original point, he saw that the stranger was still behind him, a gray hood pulled low over his forehead. At one point in the night walk, Michel passed the familiar woolen shop, never slowing his pace. He passed the windowless wall, but he could not tarry without endangering his teacher. Thus he took leave of Narbonne without even paying his respects to LeCler, though the luminous Tree of Life would forever be marked in his memory.

I was relieved to hear from Michel that my family was safe—I had not seen them now for some time—but Michel's letter cast me into a gloomy state, one soon to be made gloomier yet, for my comfortable routine was shortly interrupted by an unpleasant journey required by my service to the King.

The events preceding it gave me no warning.

Shortly after the New Year of 1526 a treaty was ratified between François and his captor, Charles of Spain. The terms of the agreement were disheartening for France: among other losses of territory, our native Provence was once again to revert to the status of an independent state and I feared my position in court might be jeopardized. But I worried needlessly, for little did I know that the treaty would never go into effect.

Behind the elaborate negotiations carried on in Madrid was this bit of maneuvering: Like a mouse in the woodwork, the King had shrewdly relayed a communiqué six months before through his sister Marguerite, who was the only person permitted to visit him during his grave illness. The communiqué declared that any treaty which the King might sign in captivity was to be pronounced null and void as contracted under duress. This artful dodge was sanctified by Pope Clement, and while the French parliament was apprised of this, the populace was not to know until the King's release had been secured. This was no simple feat, as a cruel trap lay ahead for François.

Charles had originally agreed to release his captor solely on François's word of honor—but as a guarantee, Charles now demanded the King's two oldest children as hostages.

I was told that upon hearing this François replied, "What good is a King without a kingdom?" after which he agreed to surrender his sons.

For me this agreement meant an apprenticeship in exile. I had shown devotion to the Dauphin and young Henri, so now I was to accompany the children to Spain. The Queen Mother Louise was no tyrant and I was at will to refuse, but without prompting from Uncle Léon, I sensed that in some future time my sacrifice would be rewarded. Had I known the duration of our exile ...but, of course, I could not...and so, unaware of François's plan to break the treaty, I trusted that the Spanish would treat two princes and their attendant with all possible courtesy and comfort and that before long we would all be home once again.

There were scores of brightly dressed courtiers in our traveling party, their varicolored costumes a counterfeit festivity in contrast to the somber honesty of that gray morning in March when we left Paris on the journey to Hendaye, the last town in France at the edge of the detested Spanish border.

We traveled overland slowly, my horse following a litter bearing the two princes. The lean, stark landscape offered little diversion, but once when a handsome stag appeared on a nearby hillock, I called out to Henri (who loved the hunt), "Pull aside the curtain!" His small, frightened face emerged from behind the drape, dark eyes disclosing no emotion. In a moment he had slumped back in his seat again and did not look out until we arrived at the next resting place; for Henri, there was no disguising the journey's purpose.

In fifteen days we reached Hendaye, where the princes rested within tents while attendants who would soon return to Paris began preparation for the King's reception.

The Dauphin was restless with excitement at the prospect of seeing his father for the first time in two years; he had willingly accepted the role of hostage so that his father might continue a sovereignty which would one day be his.

But Henri was indifferent to his father's reappearance. Now a sullen seven years of age, Henri had become more withdrawn over the past two years, an inturning of character many attributed to the death of his mother, Queen Claude. While she had lived, the boy depended on her quiet strength. That night, on the southern edge of France, he stared across the river and grimly awaited the morrow's exchange of himself and his brother for one royal sire.

We huddled in the river barge as the bargemen thrust their poles into the sand, sending the craft gliding away from the bank. On the Spanish shore, I saw what appeared as our reflection across the blue-green expanse. The river remained a mirror until the distance between the twin barges diminished and the enemy flag came sharply into view. There, in the center of the River Bidasoa, within a few hands' reach of each other, the two barges passed. The King gazed helplessly at our barge, his eyes sunken and dark from recent illness. He called to me as we neared each other midriver, "Take care of my sons," then to them, "I will come back for you soon."

In the mingling of small, uncaring waves he could not hear the two boys who cried out as their father shrank to a speck on the opposite bank.

I believe my presence provided some consolation to the children during the next four years. The first day in Madrid, when Spanish guards locked us into large but dreary rooms, I assessed our surroundings and set about at once to amuse the princes, hoping to raise their poor spirits and make the time pass more quickly. Though I tried my best, I never long succeeded in making them forget our predicament.

As a Christian I had been taught the saintly value of sacrifice, but it had never occurred to me to become a saint. Quite the contrary. And as our first year in Spain neared an end, I brooded that this was no way for a man to spend his prime, not when he could be in Paris enjoying perfumes rather than the stale air of hostage quarters. My muse agreed, for I was unable to wrest poetry from her that first year, perhaps because I spent my wits reciting too-familiar poetry and telling old tales to two insatiable boys.

Besides my repertoire there was little occasion for amusement inside our stone-walled chamber, which had one high window with heavy bars set deep into thick stone, through which the children could see only if I stood upon a stool and hoisted them one at a time onto my shoulders.

Once when I lifted Henri until his eyes reached the rim of the window, he called down, "There's a glorious sunset tonight. The sky is smoky gold, like a topaz, with streaks of purple in it!" His feet were planted firmly on my shoulders, his hands clasped around the rusted iron window-bars to give us both support.

"Alain," he sighed, "I wish you could stand on my back and see outside, but I'm too weak to hold you."

Only once did the Dauphin mount my shoulders to look from the window. He peered into the courtyard and reported that soon there would be a celebration, for he could see the seats and colored bunting which foretold a tournament. Then suddenly he lost interest in the world outside our cell and cried with fright, "Father told you to take care of me. What if I fall and break my neck?"

"Then I'll be Dauphin," Henri said dryly.

"Set me down," the Dauphin shrieked, certain of a conspiracy between us.

I set him firmly on the stone floor, angry with myself for apparently showing preference to Henri. This must have spurred the Dauphin's fear. At that time I had not yet mastered the telling look in my eyes, the last note of plain honesty which signaled to a lady or a young prince that I cared for them greatly, or not at all.

The only outing permitted us was attendance at Mass each Sunday when, as the only lay worshipers, we were led by guards into a small chapel within the fortress. Once in those four years we were granted confession, though I admit I did not insist. I had not confessed to a priest since assuming my position in court, but in that dreary fortress—as if I'd been given a taste of purgatory before being cast into hell—I found myself craving the blessing and absolution of a universal church, a church which enfolds Frenchman and Spaniard alike.

On that single occasion of atonement, at Christmastime of our second year, I gave my confession to the priest in very rusty Latin and afterward wondered at how refreshed my soul felt for its unburdening.

The Dauphin refused to accompany us, claiming that his father and Aunt Marguerite were in sympathy with the Reformers.

"I think the old Church is nearly dead," he said, "and when I am King I shall favor the new."

"What is wrong with the old?" asked Henri. "The past is better than this, isn't it? What's to look forward to? The Mass is always the same, now and forever. The incense and bells and glass windows are old things I can trust."

"How can you even make confession?" the Dauphin sneered. "You only know little boys' Latin so you won't be able to speak to the priest. But I've had one more year of Latin than you, so if I wanted to I could give confession—but I don't want to."

"Then you are a worse sinner than I," Henri said, "for I am willing but cannot, while you are able but will not."

"My little brother is becoming a hair-splitting theologian," the Dauphin yawned. "Pity poor France if ever I fall and break my neck."

During the years of our captivity, while we waited eagerly for the King's return, the King concerned himself mainly with his own recovery, which consisted primarily of a dalliance with Anne de Heilly de Pisseleu.

Pope Clement, as expected, had absolved François from his oath taken in Madrid. Upon receiving word that the treaty was annulled, Charles raged that François was no gentleman and that according to the agreement, he should return to prison at once (which of course the King was unwilling to do). This resulted in our being relocated to quarters even lower in the fortress, to a windowless, moldy chamber where we fell asleep at night to the sound of rats scurrying about in the dark. We no longer were escorted to Mass on Sundays, which even the Dauphin regretted, for by this time he could appreciate the pungent smell of incense and the feel of velvet cushions.

Our worsened situation wasn't Charles's only act of revenge for the broken treaty: He sent his army to sack Rome and ordered the imprisonment of Pope Clement. François was bound to defend the Pope in his hour of need, and in acknowledgment of this obligation, the King of France challenged the King of Spain to a duel. Of course it was unthinkable for two monarchs to risk their lives in a single combat even though outrage had followed outrage, so another solution had to be found, and while the flamboyant King of France pressed on loudly in his contest of words against the King of Spain, the Queen Mother quietly negotiated with Marguerite of Austria, aunt to Charles, and between them an agreement was forged. This new treaty, proposed to both François and Charles in lieu of the shattered Treaty of Madrid, was deemed acceptable by both parties. After four years in Spain, we were soon to be free.

The same flat, blue-green river faced us at Fontarabia; the same mirror image of a barge appeared across the water, but no one was seated within it and this time the other barge did not stir. Instead, as we crossed the Bidasoa, we saw a crowd of our own countrymen and women, all richly dressed, their faces smiling in welcome as we approached the shore. But as we neared the riverbank we could see that while it was a noble party greeting us, the King was not among them.

"He would not trouble himself to meet us," Henri said angrily, holding back disappointed tears.

"Would you want a monarch to risk harm?" the Dauphin said as we stepped from the barge and into the welcoming throng. Instinctively the Dauphin stood erect before his father's subjects; Henri appeared disturbed by the confusion and held onto my hand with desperation at first, and only did he loosen his grip when a certain woman approached. I did not recognize her, but I noticed Henri staring intently. She was indeed beautiful, though nearer my age than his; in fact, she was old enough to be Henri's mother but in no other way did she resemble the plain Queen Claude, this woman on the shore so slender, graceful and distantly cool.

II

CONCERNING LESSONS LEARNED IN PRISON, AND THE WISDOM OF EXILE

THE Seine sparkled in midday sunlight as we crossed the ancient bridge lined precariously with shops that joined the left bank to the Ile de la Cité. Young Henri was the first to notice the architectural modifications of the Louvre, which had been restored during our absence; I wondered what other changes we might find.

The King received us with great ceremony, and for three days and nights he provided banquets and dancers, musicians, jesters and clowns. Continuous sporting matches filled the afternoon programs. I was fatigued by the constant activity but assumed the young princes enjoyed themselves, though I knew each celebrated in a manner befitting his respective nature. Closer observation proved me wrong.

I, of course, watched the elegant noblemen and their beautiful ladies as they bowed and turned to the music in a sumptuous swirl of fabric. I devoured the hues of the gowns: saffron yellow, indigo blue of a starless night, the vibrance of Armenian scarlet. Throats shimmered with Egyptian emeralds, clusters of deep red rubies, ropes of luminous pearls. I could hardly contain my joy.

But then I noticed Henri's sullen face. His only hours of happiness since our return were those of the hunt, when he was transformed into the congenial boy we remembered from before his mother's death, before the ordeal of the Alcazar prison in Madrid. The Dauphin may have thrilled to the pageantry, but young Henri sat stone-faced and grim; it may have been too early to judge, but already some people said that in Spain Henri had become as gloomy as a Spaniard.

Other disturbing thoughts tormented the young prince, for while the rest of us mindlessly followed the entertainers' routines, Henri brooded upon the announcement of his betrothal to the niece of Pope Clement VII. Her name was Catherine, of the Florentine Medici family, and the girl was reported to be thin and short with heavy features and the unattractive, protruding Medici eyes. Thus far Henri's life had granted him few pleasures, and none appeared on the horizon. His brother François would inherit the throne while he would always remain the second son and, due to his subdued nature, never the one to enjoy his father's attention.

Yet Henri shared his father's love of the hunt and from an early age he took great interest in the King's great architectural projects. In particular, Henri was fascinated by an old lodge located in the countryside at Fontainebleau, a crumbling ruin which the King had discovered one day while riding. It is said that on that day the King commanded his entire entourage to halt while he dismounted, then he spent the entire afternoon exploring the abandoned rooms of some long-dead feudal lord. True to his impulsive nature and penchant for ambitious undertakings, the King thereupon vowed to transform the ruin into a royal hunting lodge.

Fortunately for Henri, a grand hunt was planned at Fontainebleau to crown the children's homecoming, and in one rare hour of intimacy, Henri and his royal father would ride their horses to a lather, side by side.

*   *   *

As I settled into my new quarters (for my old room had been occupied by another man during the past two years) I was handed a packet of letters that had arrived in my absence. One was from my family, informing me of the birth of my first nephew. The other two were from Michel.

August,
1527

I have lately been in the city of Carcassonne on this discouraging sojourn through Languedoc. On whichever byway or rutted street I traveled in Carcassonne, I passed a niche; within each niche stood a statue, for that city had assembled an army of small saints to wage battle against the pestilence.

Michel's reputation as healer had spread in the rampant manner of provincial gossip, so that upon his arrival in the well-fortified city, the people were disposed to welcome him inside their walls as if he had been dispatched by Saint Adrian himself.

But in Carcassonne as in Narbonne, the true gift of healing was ill-received by the local doctors. He was dismayed, for the initial acceptance deluded Michel into believing that the city might provide a safe haven, since he was greatly fatigued and must somehow gather the strength to continue his work. He intended to remain only a few more days, after discovering not only that resentment seethed in the city, but also that Carcassonne provided no access to the teachings he sought. Thus he departed for Toulouse, leaving his patients to less skilled, less caring hands.

The second letter, which was dated in the spring of 1528, was more hopeful:

The city of Toulouse shall be the final place in what has seemed an endless journey, for here I have found a second home.

At first I arranged for a modest room at an inn, as is my custom, but within the month a wealthy banker insisted on providing me with fine lodgings in gratitude for successful treatment of his young wife.

The banker had pleaded, "You were sent by the saints—do not refuse my hospitality." By so doing, he hoped to ensure the future welfare of his family.

Michel accepted the offer, although wary of comfort and even more suspicious of gifts, so intent was he on remaining free of the yoke of indebtedness.

Yet under the protective mantle of this banker named Dupre, Michel's weakened health was fully restored. He was allotted a generous suite of rooms for his personal use, and the service of an old housekeeper to tend his needs. Each night after making the round of his patients, he would return to his quarters on the Rue de la Triperie, where in his absence the old woman had dusted the chairs and chests and smoothed his bed. If the night was cool, a bedwarmer would be heating the linens, and a mug of spiced wine would be waiting on the reading table beside the trimmed oil lamp. In such an atmosphere of domestic comfort, Michel made great strides in his work. At last he was able to procure a copy of Ptolemy's *Tetrabiblos,* and once again he turned to the study of astrology by night, in the privacy of his room.

Coupled with his diurnal tasks as healer, this routine of work and study strengthened Michel's understanding of the link between planetary models and the frailties of men. Once again he found himself receptive to secret potencies of herbs, and at times he was compelled to administer curious compounds; thus did he discover a remarkable remedy for the pestilence.

The patient who inspired this remedy was a young priest. Michel's first three attempts brought no improvement. Then, as he swabbed the dark pustules with an ointment of little efficacy, he allowed his thoughts to wander as if seeking relief from the discouragement of the work.

Michel had told me earlier of the process whereby images came forth and revolved before him, as in a dream. So it was while he tended this patient; in a daydream he imagined the legs and arms of the stricken

cleric as limbs of a sapling. Other vernal images played
upon his mind: fragments of memory, a reverie of ferns
and blossoms. Then Michel heard a phrase, as though
a human voice had spoken, though no one but the unconscious patient was in the room: "Rose of Sharon,
Damascus Rose." The phrase repeated, echoed in his
mind, and thus he knew that roses were essential for
the cure.

Though the prescription was simple, finding these
ingredients was not.

"You seek the unattainable," he was told as he combed
the shops in search of rose petals. "Your roses are not
to be found in any garden in France at this time of
year," a flower vendor in the marketplace told him.

Not easily dissuaded, so definite was the command,
Michel finally found a sympathetic stranger who recommended dried petals in place of fresh, and the name
of a perfumer who could provide them. At last he stood
in the perfumer's workshop among vials and vats of
scents. The man was overjoyed to see a customer, so
little business had been conducted in recent months.
From inside a cabinet he removed a large coffer; beneath the lid lay thousands of withered brown petals,
indistinguishable now, though once they had glowed
with color.

The perfumer thought Michel's request odd, but he
agreed to grind the petals into powder and to press the
powder into lozenges which could slowly dissolve in the
patient's mouth.

That night Michel sat through another vigil; when
one lozenge was gone, he placed another beneath the
tongue of the young priest. By dawn there were signs
of improvement, though Michel did not consider the
treatment a success until another month had passed
and the man was at last able to walk in the room un-
aided.

The perfumer, however, did not wait until the rose
lozenge had been proven. Within a few days of the doctor's visit to his workshop, he began touting packets
containing a dozen lozenges as "the famous rose pills
of Doctor Nostradamus." Partly due to this hawking,

the cure of roses was a much-heralded treatment, one
which seemed to render all other methods obsolete.
Other physicians claimed that the plague had run its
course, though perhaps this skepticism was merely a
jealous outcry. The result, in any case, was that Michel
now saw the pestilence at bay, and decided to depart
for Montpellier to complete examinations for the physician's degree. He wrote:

> Four years have passed since I left the college of
> medicine. My travels have taken me throughout our
> Provençal homeland and to cities in Languedoc which
> otherwise I would not have seen. I have been given
> gold by those who could afford to pay me, and I have
> gained a reputation for beneficence among those who
> could not. My old mule is not equal to the five-day
> journey, and so I shall leave him with my host to do
> less strenuous tasks.

> Tonight, in anticipation of tomorrow's departure, I
> have been thinking of the past, for a small incident
> this very evening evoked a memory of our childhood.

> As I sat before the fire grate, the housekeeper called
> my name. I sat up with a start and knew I had been
> dozing. She offered me a sweet set upon a saucer, a
> pale morsel of pastry baked for the occasion of my
> leaving Toulouse. I bit into the crust and recognized
> the flavor I had loved best as a child, the comforting
> sweetness of a pastry glazed with quince jam.

> I regard this as an omen, a cycle of return to earlier
> times. Perhaps, my friend, we must revisit our past,
> the better to understand our future.

I had only finished reading the second letter when
a message was delivered from my Uncle Léon, request-
ing that I visit him at my earliest leave.

The following day, since the hunting party to Fontainebleau was planned and my presence was not required, I borrowed a horse and rode to Léon's home on
Rue Lafitte.

*   *   *

The impertinent valet led me to the study, and as Uncle Léon and I faced each other for the first time in four years, I was amused to see no perceptible sign of aging. No doubt he had kept up his rejuvenating program of intrigue despite my absence. We embraced; he ordered me a glass of cognac.

"A libation, to thank the gods for your safe return," he said.

"You have finally answered my question about religion," I said, warming the amber liquid by cupping my palm around the glass, "for you are neither Protestant nor Catholic—you are a pagan."

Léon laughed heartily and I joined him, whereupon he noted that in four years I had not overcome the vulgar habit of laughing at my own jokes.

"Let us raise a toast to our widower-King's new bride, Eleanor, and to the worth of your recent ordeal, though it seemed pointless at the time, I am sure. Now you must tell me *all*."

"There is little to recount," I said. "I saw only the countryside between Madrid and Fontarabia; the city I glimpsed only once in passing each direction, and then it was dusk. The only Spaniards I saw were jailers and a priest, and the food, I can tell you, was terrible! Tasteless gruel, stale bread, an occasional bit of greasy meat. They kept us from the mariner's disease by including an occasional handful of kumquats. I have had such an appetite since my return that surely I shall burst from my tunic within the fortnight."

"Perhaps you would prefer to forego the roast lamb and baby onions which my cook has prepared." He feigned a sniff. "It smells as though it is just now done to a turn. Pity."

"No," I protested, "of course I will dine. Surely my appetite is a sign of returning vitality."

Uncle Léon pressed me further for information gleaned during those (to me) lost years; specifically he inquired about the characters of the young princes. He had a way of extracting intelligence where there appeared to be none.

"Now that you ask, I did notice inclinations in each of them, for the intensity of our confinement rendered traits in sharp contrast. I will spare you the details and offer instead a conclusion: if the Dauphin ascends to the throne there will be no discontinuity of policy—but if for any reason Henri should succeed..."

Léon's face brightened with anticipation. "You see a possibility of major change?"

"Yes," I replied, "for in Spain I learned this: young Henri lives in the past."

During the next two years, I gave little thought to how Henri might alter policy should he become king, for Henri demanded little of me and therefore was not on my mind; meanwhile, the Dauphin required my full attention. In the course of my duties I became attendant of the Dauphin's wardrobe; I guaranteed that tailors completed his sumptuous garments in time for this or that festival or investiture; I saw to it that his hose were tinted to harmonize with each ensemble. And beyond concern for special-occasion garments, I assured a vast selection of daily clothing, for His Highness changed garments, according to his mood, several times each day.

You may envision me as a royal lackey with little life of my own, but this is not true. Though the future of my position depended upon service to the princes' needs, I nonetheless found the time and the means to advance my career and also to cultivate the affection of court beauties.

The King was widely known for his dalliances; it was a spirit which pervaded the court. Thus, while it may seem that a man like myself had little to offer a woman, yet I was desired. At the time desirability meant comeliness enhanced with talent. Immodestly I may say I possessed these qualities to a greater degree than many of my peers. My mastery of the lute and my verses were beginning to be appreciated among the members of the court, and so favored was I by one lady-in-waiting that through her sponsorship I found myself in the courtiers' inner circle. This is how it came about:

One afternoon as I waited by the grass court for the Dauphin to finish his tennis game, I noticed a splendid young lady looking in my direction. I saw this several times during the game. After its conclusion she walked toward me.

"You are Alain Saint-Germain," she said in a voice both confident and coy. "You are the man who cared for the princes in Madrid."

"I am he."

"I have also heard that you compose love songs."

"That also is true."

"Then tell me, are your songs based on truth or are they mere conjecture?"

"To me they are true," I replied, "but a poet's truth is not the same as everyman's."

Just then, someone called her name; she turned and waved the other young man away, and directing her green eyes at me again she said, "Have you a song about a courtier's lady? If so, perhaps you would sing it for a few of us tomorrow night."

"No, mademoiselle, I have not," I began, then intuition made me bold and I added, "for until today, I have not loved a court lady."

She continued to smile without a flickering of her eyelids, much less a blush, at my bare confession, as though my reply was expected. I decided this lovely woman—so fragile to behold, with a voice as delicate as a small silver bell—was in fact a strong and cunning creature and not one I should treat too gently. Perhaps she and not I would give the lesson in love.

I wondered how to suggest an assignation but she took the task from my hands. As the tennis match closed with the Dauphin as winner, I felt a tug at my sleeve and looked down to see a page. He thrust a folded note into my hand, then disappeared. The note said she would meet me at the coach house that evening at sunset. I glanced to where the Lady Yvette sat across the grassy court. We smiled; it was agreed.

Pink and gray clouds of a spring sunset gave forth muted light, but due to a thick stand of trees around the coach house it was already dark inside when I slipped through unlocked doors.

"Here," she called.

My eyes became accustomed to the gloom as I made my way cautiously toward her voice, past the shadowy forms of coaches whose gold leaf would daze my sight, were we in daylight.

"Why did you choose the coach house?" I asked.

"My brother is head coachman and it is dinner hour for him and the men. We have only this one hour, so let us not waste it."

Now I could clearly see the coach and Lady Yvette, who was buried in a comforter to cover her legs, and soon I discovered that she wore only a long, hooded cloak and riding boots which slipped off easily and soon lay in a heap upon the floor.

The hour sped by, so lost were we in our pleasure. The coach contained the warm thick air of our love. It was only by luck that the coachmen were late in returning, for we had just slipped out the carriage house door when men swaggered around the corner of the building, laughing loudly and belching after an evening meal. We took refuge in the stand of trees, away from the moon's rising light.

"You will come tomorrow night?" she asked. I, misunderstanding her intention, interrupted her with a kiss as my reply, for this seemed appropriate.

"No, to read your poetry," she said impatiently, as though I were a foolish child. "You are to recite for my friends, remember?"

"Yes, of course," I said, feeling dull, as though my mind was still beneath the coverlet.

"Good-bye for now," she said, with a charming softness the lady could summon at will. "Perhaps tomorrow evening you will have a new song to sing."

I watched her leave and waited until she turned into a doorway before departing my hiding place among the trees. Such good fortune, I thought, breathing in the smell of early mist on spring bark. My thoughts wandered from the lady's arms ahead to the next evening, when I would make my first appearance in court: this time not as attendant, but as poet and musician. If they favored me, I would not be first to make such an ascent, but I would be one of few.

On that evening, attired in my best tunic and with

the beautiful Lady Yvette at my side, I sang my love songs before the men and women of the court. Before beginning I strummed the lute, testing strings for tone, while I explained that my songs should be regarded as stages in the understanding of love wherein a man finds each love to be finer than the one before, much as the alchemists turn base metal into gold.

I sang of a young man's first love, of his tentative steps into an unknown land.

I sang of a student's love, at once deep yet shallow.

I sang of love for a married woman, of the danger and delight.

I sang (though not from experience) of the comforting love of a man's own wife.

And finally I praised the love of a courtly Lady, whose grace and flawless beauty proves her the paragon of her kind.

She clasped my hand when the song's last note faded to silence.

"He is a treasure," her friend whispered, casting me an inviting smile.

"His songs are pretty, but he is no philosopher," sneered an elegant young man who sat with one leg draped over the carved arm of a massive chair. "Surely first love must be purer, its motives more sincere, than those of later loves; hence the analogy breaks down: first love cannot be considered like the base metal which so-called alchemists turn to gold."

"I agree," said another man, "and to attack the analogy further, our poet—who is *definitely* not a philosopher—should be told that he is quite far from gold when loving a lady of the court. Here he will only stumble upon a cache of fool's gold."

The other men joined in the hilarity; my companion did not let go her hand, but it felt so lifeless that I would rather she had. I, stranded in a sea of ridicule, had no support forthcoming from my mistress, so it remained to defend myself and Yvette's honor as well. Miserable, with a dozen sets of eyes staring disdainfully, I sat near to suffocation in my tight velvet tunic and tried to devise a position.

Then I recalled the song I had written for Michel. I

had almost forgotten it, a poem not written from my own life and memory, but from the spring of my love for him, in an effort to grasp his often unfathomable ideals. Now, though my mouth was dry as linen, I managed to speak with what I hoped would seem a confident air:

"You are right, of course," I said, "and in anticipation of this objection, I have another song which shall set the analogy straight again. For compared to a higher love which leads man to his own soul, even first love is base and merely the first step in one's journey."

When it was sung and when I saw the approval and admiration I had aimed for, I then rose, took my lute, bowed and left the room. That evening, at least, I had the final note.

When I was summoned by the King next day, I assumed he had been informed of my performance the night before. I had nothing to fear; this audience could only be to my benefit. Nonetheless I was trembling when I entered his counsel chamber. There he addressed me briefly while I prostrated myself before him.

"Are you familiar with the *Book of the Courtier* written by a Florentine called Castiglione?" he asked.

"No, Your Majesty."

"I suggest you familiarize yourself with its contents. I recommend this only to increase your considerable natural judgment in matters of court life. It has come to my attention that you have a gift for adapting yourself to situations. Now I come to the point: my son Henri is not adaptable. Both his eye and his appetite for court life are dull. I desire that you sharpen them. The Dauphin is progressing well and has a certain temperament for conducting himself as royal-born, but Henri fails in this and soon he is to be married. Therefore, with the impending wedding, this lesson is urgent. I am appointing you as his personal *valet de chambre*. You are to engage him in conversation. Suggest…certain 'activities.' Use your proven ingenuity."

"Your Majesty," I said, overwhelmed, "I will do all I can."

* * *

When I had heard from Michel in 1529, he wrote that while the students of Montpellier had greeted his return with camaraderie and respect, the professors had greeted him only with scorn.

In particular, the old doctor who (he reminded me) had once bored me with the anatomy lesson, had said to him: "Ah, the famous 'Doctor' Nostradamus. And have the years of plague endowed you with wisdom, young man? More wisdom, I pray, than when we saw you last."

Michel was then twenty-seven, and ten years older than the youngest students in the college of medicine. He resented being regarded as an untried youth by this professor who had remained cloistered within the walls of the college while his students set forth to live in hardship and risk their lives to aid thousands of stricken countrymen.

Michel knew there were many illnesses he had had no occasion to treat, but at the time this seemed to him a minor point. He was still buoyed by his victory in the field, and though tempted to tell the professor that he had succeeded in a far greater test, he decided to humble himself until the examination was complete and he had been awarded the physician's degree.

"I have much to learn," Michel said modestly.

"Then let us see how much you do *not* know."

The austerities Michel now imposed upon himself in order to prepare for the remaining examinations would have been impossible four years ago, before he had known the sleepless days and nights when relenting would have meant handing an easy win to Death. In a small room shared with another student, Michel pored over his books, sleeping only two or three hours a night. To keep himself awake as he studied, he kept cold water, small stones or slices of turnip in his mouth. Often he disagreed with the time-worn theories, and now that he had proof to support his own ideas, it required discipline and caution to withhold the controversial answers he longed to give during the examinations; carefully he phrased his replies to fit the examiner's expectations until he possessed the graduate cap and the book of Hippocrates. Finally he was offered a teaching position on the Montpellier faculty; now, Michel believed his voice would be heard.

On the first day behind the podium, though Montpellier tradition forbade student discussion in the lecture room, Michel astonished his students by announcing that they were free to formulate critical questions regarding such iron-clad procedures as the letting of blood and the examination of urine. "If there appears to be another procedure, I shall tell you why it will or will not succeed; if I cannot tell you, I shall find an answer; if I cannot find an answer, I shall tell you no one knows."

The wave of murmurs that followed Michel's announcement gave him satisfaction; he would shake these student-physicians from complacence, force them to seek truth for themselves rather than accept the threadbare theories of the professors.

He waited. No questions were asked. Even at the insistence of Doctor Nostradamus, the Montpellier students were bound by fear of committing infractions.

Michel was summoned before the dean.

"So, you think your devices are persuasive here, as if the college is some rustic schoolroom," said his superior. "I can understand that you are—shall we say—'unfamiliar' with the issues of the day after your long absence, but I must inform you that we at Montpellier, as well as our peers in Avignon and Lyons, are all watched closely by agents of the Sorbonne. My dear Doctor Nostredame, to be a heretic who wears the robe of Hippocrates is no safer than to be one wearing the robes of Saint Peter. The latest victims of the Sorbonne are not renegade priests but the readers of the Royal College, men of humanist letters."

"How can this be? The King established the Royal College and made many of the appointments himself," Michel countered.

"Yes, the King sympathizes with paganism, as we all know. The cultures of Greece and Rome are the inspiration for much of his costly architecture. But the

Sorbonne does not want its authority undermined by myths of dead civilizations."

"My views on medicine have nothing to do with religion. I am faithful to the Church."

"Your methods have been likened to witchcraft. You will admit they deviate from the Aristotelian system in which we organize our thinking into categories of genus and species. Your ideas defy logic and reason! I've heard that you prescribe some magic talisman to your patients."

"A lozenge of rose powder."

"And I know you tried to provoke our students into rebellion against their superiors. How do you think this is regarded? It is regarded as heresy! In short, if you value your position at Montpellier, you must abide by our policies."

"I value my position less than a single shrunken flower."

"Then I presume you have alternate plans, young man; there is no longer room for you here."

As my fortunes after the years of exile in Spain took a better turn, so did Michel's after his dismissal from Montpellier. In 1532, convinced that some meaning was to be gleaned from the cycle of return to past experiences, he now set out on a return journey to the cities he had visited during the plague years. He was in the prime of his years at twenty-nine and confident that his reputation would smooth the way. He wrote to me at this time:

As I travel back through time, to Avignon, Carcassonne, to Narbonne and Toulouse, I forget the harsh words of the dean. Happy to be rid of the dank stone buildings, the musty straw of classroom floors, I ride through the countryside as free of care as any man could be.

He enjoyed the hearty fare of roadside inns and listened to travelers' tales. He journeyed as one of many vagabonds, for the roads of France carried many men who traveled, and many like himself who had only the vaguest of goals; all strangers who joined nightly in the wayside inns and recounted tales to each other.

Evenings in the crowded inns and peaceful days astride his mule were only a small portion of this time in Michel's life, for along this retracing of steps he could not avoid confronting illness when his presence became known. Most were common cases and not the deadly disease of earlier years, nor was his work heralded as miraculous, for death kept a distance. Now, when he departed a sickbed, Michel returned to cobbled streets bustling with everyday routine: the sound of vendors, of children, of chore carts. He almost forgot the sight of a death cart's lumbering wheels, the sight of spectral tumbleweeds drifting through desolate streets.

His work earned Michel a modest living and simple satisfactions, the pleasure of peaceful days. He tended few extraordinary ailments and thus ordinary remedies sufficed; rarely did he ponder as in the past, nor did he need draw upon inner resources in order to heal. Thus, after almost a decade of battle against disease and doctrine, as student, itinerant healer, professor of medicine, Michel de Nostredame was now a physician quite comfortable with his irregular practice.

For three years he had lived unchallenged and content. By relinquishing his position at Montpellier, Michel thought he had left behind the intellectual arena, but in fact his reputation as a man of independent mind eventually reached the ears of a noted scholar and botanist, who invited Michel to reside in the town of Agen.

November,
1533

I have at last found a city which tempts me to establish residence, as well as a patron under whose guidance my work will surely flourish. His name is César Scaliger.

Of course I knew of Scaliger, whose name was oft mentioned during my student years. His repute was due mainly to his violent retort to an essay of Erasmus—an essay in which Erasmus had criticized the popular use of Ciceronian Latin. Scaliger, on the other hand, claimed (with all the passion of an Italian defending the former glory of Rome) that Ciceronian Latin was the purest language in its most exalted form. Scaliger was a man who loved debate.

After Michel had been a guest in César's home for several weeks and had announced his decision to remain in Agen and there establish his medical practice, César proposed another course of action, one which I suspect he had in mind even before extending the original invitation to Michel months before. He advised that Michel marry, and to this end he recommended Madeleine Belleau, a young woman of good family who, he assured Michel, would be a virtuous wife.

Before I learned of Michel's betrothal, other nuptial preparations occupied my attention. The wedding of Henri and Catherine de Medici was celebrated in Marseilles, where it began poorly with the two shy children barely acknowledging each other's presence. Of course Henri had exhibited little prior interest in girls, despite my prompting, while Catherine had other reasons for showing shyness: she was the frightened, abused offspring of a noble family now in decline. Orphaned at only one month of age when her mother succumbed to syphilis, as had her father only months before, the child Catherine was raised in a convent, constantly guarded against those who wished her death as an end to the Medici line. Though her childhood was not conducive to the gaining of confidence, Catherine was nonetheless well-mannered and well-meaning, but it remained that she was also quiet and singularly unattractive, two qualities which did not go half the length to win Henri's heart.

And when the bridal party had returned to Paris, the new Duchess d'Orleans faced a cold reception, for in her entourage she made the mistake of bringing too many Florentines, which aroused the suspicions of an already mistrusting people. Her fine manners failed to charm the citizens of Paris; they called her "the Florentine" and "the shopkeeper's daughter" with a sour inflection, little appreciating her superior education and excellent taste.

When the bride was given in marriage by her uncle, the Pontiff Clement, King François had vowed to impose harsher restrictions upon the Protestants as a way of honoring the alliance between Rome and France. Until the year before, the King had maintained a policy of tolerance toward the Reformers, for he preferred to expend energy in pursuit of pleasure and in the furthering of his architectural projects rather than in chasing after heretics.

His change of stance caused me considerable concern for, with my duties as attendant to the royal groom now behind me, I wished to attend Michel's forthcoming wedding in Agen and also to pay a brief visit to my family who were only a few days' ride farther south— and yet it had recently been reported that Huguenot factions clustered in that area, and I did not wish to incite the suspicions of those eyes that watched constantly for heresy. Assured by my Uncle Léon that physical proximity to rebellion would not compromise me, I prepared to attend Michel's wedding.

The journey from Paris to Agen required fifteen days upon horseback, and I arrived at the home of Michel de Nostredame just after midday.

He opened the door as I was wiping dust from the brim of my hat. When he saw me, a smile spread slowly across his thin face, its high cheekbones, the familiar lineaments which I had not seen for ten years, now edged with firm maturity. We embraced in the doorway and I glanced over his shoulder into the house where two older men and a beautiful young woman were sitting at table in a room redolent with the scent of spiced meat.

"You've arrived in time to join our supper," Michel said in his taut voice, projected as always in carefully chosen words. "The servant will bring you a basin of water," he said, adding with a friendly taunt, "and we'll save you a scrap of meat, if you hurry."

I was shown to a room, and the porcelain bowl was soon delivered. I dipped my hands into the basin, splashed cool water onto my dusty face, then hurriedly changed into a fresh tunic and soft leather boots as readily as the infernal hooks and laces would allow.

When I entered the room, Michel led me by the arm toward Madeleine. As introductions were made, Michel clasped the young woman's hand so tightly that her modest smile became pinched with discomfort, though she tried to hide it.

She was a slender girl, clad in a blue-gray dress, with long hair the color of pale gold. As I approached the table, I saw with surprise that her eyes were of the same serene color as her gown. She offered her hand, and I recall most vividly the exchange of tender smiles between her and Michel; it called to mind a line of a poem I had once written: "when in your eyes I see my gaze, as in a mirror."

Here in this remote town is a lady worthy of my friend's ideals, I thought. She is as fine and beautiful as any pampered woman of the court, and more virtuous by far. I wondered that Michel had found her in spite of himself.

As I was marveling over this unexpected creature (and fast forgetting the picture I had painted in my mind of a woman rustic and plain), I saw Madeleine frown slightly then whisper to Michel, who stooped close to hear. His face flushed and he muttered, "Of course, forgive me," then let go her hand that she might offer it to me, as was the custom. I found the small hand warmer and more vital than I expected, for at first glance she did appear frail, her skin so pale and translucent one could see the blood rushing to its surface at the faintest flicker of emotion, the fine veins showing blue along her temple where it met her smooth golden hair. Her delicate mouth curved in a wan, almost somnolent smile.

This rush of impressions was cut short as Michel introduced me to the three men: Madeleine's father, her uncle and César Scaliger. The three men each clasped my hand, then returned to some heated discussion which my arrival had interrupted.

I sat beside Michel, who discreetly informed me that I would meet Madeleine's mother at some other time.

Today she was unable to join us due to an unspecified illness.

"The poor woman is of a weak constitution; that is, she prefers to remain at home tended by servants in her lilac-scented bedchamber."

This remark gave me cause to wonder if the delicate Madeleine might one day follow in her mother's ways.

"Is there no explanation for the woman's illness?" I asked.

"I could give a diagnosis, but she is soon to be my mother-in-law, so I restrain myself from declaring that it is nothing but her imagination. On the other hand I refuse to give the phantom illness a false name and dignify her sham, so the lady calls me a charlatan. She says, 'You have cured hundreds of people of the dreaded plague, but you cannot treat one poor, sickly woman such as I.'" He sighed. "She is tedious, but I have learned to ignore her. Fortunately Scaliger has wholly endorsed our betrothal, and Madeleine's father is convinced I will be a perfect husband for his only child."

I had arrived two days before the ceremony, and after only one evening in Scaliger's presence I had summarized him as a man of great learning and extremely narrow mind.

"Here is a prime case of impulse to self-display," Scaliger said angrily as he burst through Michel's door the next afternoon. He had just returned from the book fair in Lyons, and in his hand he held a copy of Rabelais's *Gargantua,* purchased at the fair.

It appeared to me that the doctor was angered by a single fact that had little to do with the content of Rabelais's work: no printer in Lyons was even slightly interested in publishing César's latest essay.

Confirming my conclusion, he raged, "The printers in Lyons told me the only books which bring profit are romances, inflammatory pamphlets or tales of magic and marvels, while scholarly works do not even pay for printers' costs. The public clamors for this coarse and disgusting verbiage," he said, dropping the Rabelais book on the table. "Only at the promise of being shocked, aroused or mystified do shoppers spring to open their purses."

I picked up *Gargantua* and began leafing through its pages. I knew Rabelais wrote as an anti-cleric in a time when the Church was under harsh criticism. Rabelais's iconoclastic pen scorned revered institutions, including the rite of marriage, and men like Michel who revered woman as the chaste bride personified by the image of the Virgin. Mocking such a notion, Rabelais reveled in writing tales of cuckoldry.

"His writing deeply offends me," said Michel who, at thirty-one years of age, was awed by the sacrament in which he would participate on the morrow. Since our student days in Avignon he had held to the ideal of a woman whose love would lead him not to disillusionment but who would inspire in him a quest for spiritual perfection.

"The man is despicable," Scaliger seethed. "He panders to base minds, to those who desire to read of excreta, debauchery, sacrilege. Appropriately, he expresses himself in the vulgar tongue of the street peddler. Since both the content of his writing and its linguistic form are detestable, I see no justification for the publication of his work."

"But his sentiments are those of our time," I argued, "as is his choice of the popular form of language, the tongue of living Frenchmen. And while I am faithful to Our Lady, the Church," I continued with slightly exaggerated piety, "yet I am also in sympathy with Rabelais's playful criticism of Church practices, for it seems to me that if the Church is to survive, then it must be reformed from within."

Of course, once I had opened my mouth I regretted my rashness. How could I argue with this learned man?

"Criticism of the Church—what does a courtier know of intellectual criticism?" Scaliger sneered, attacking my position with relish. "Rabelais's work is no call to reform but only the work of a writer who feigns a critical attitude to justify his vulgar outpourings. Are you familiar with his passage on sacred relics?" Scaliger asked, taking the copy of *Gargantua* from my hands.

"No, I am not," I replied, fearing the debate would

turn to his favor at the moment he began to cite specific details, for my own defense was but a vague recollection of opinions gathered here and there. Nonetheless, I held my ground as he read the passage. It *was* obscene—about sacred bones from unspeakable parts of the body, a bit of "sacred shroud" covered with "revered snot." I could hardly contain my laughter and said, "I find the story amusing."

I noticed Michel shifting his body in discomfort, as his two friends locked horns. No doubt he ached to offer an ameliorating opinion; perhaps he refrained from respect for the limits of our two-man combat.

"Your choice of a word such as 'amusement' proves you are not accustomed to serious discussion," Scaliger said, adding, "indeed, perhaps you are incapable of it."

Turning to Michel he said, "Your friend is not without charm, as courtiers are bred to be. But with due respect for your long friendship with this man—and as I value our newly found one—I would prefer to conclude this discussion before it turns into travesty. Good evening, sirs," he said, rising at once and in the same motion signaling his servant. He then nodded to us brusquely and departed, leaving Michel and me alone, silent before the dying fire in the grate.

"For all his brilliance, Scaliger is blinded by certain prejudices," Michel remarked when we were alone again.

"How can a man of such reputation be so narrow? How can you stomach his stubbornness?" I asked.

Michel sighed and said, "I was perplexed at first, wondering how I could retain my integrity yet remain in his favor. Agen is a pleasant place to live, and my opportunities here are unique as the protégé of a famed man who was formerly the physician to the Bishop of Agen. I have resolved this dilemma, Alain, by presenting arguments only within the limits of César's own beliefs; in the guise of argument I construct variations of César's own point of view."

"I will pray for the preservation of your ideals, my friend."

"My ideals? What of your own?" Michel asked. "I refuse to believe you live solely for your own amusement, as Scaliger accused you of tonight."

"Well, beauty is one ideal which must earn your respect, judging by your bride-to-be. So you see, we share the same ideal after all: a love of the beautiful."

"Appearance is what you mistake for beauty," he said. "I seek a quality which cannot fade nor die."

"You must face the facts, Michel; your lady-love will someday grow old."

"I see beyond such changes. A beautiful woman is not the sea itself, but only a tributary leading to the larger expanse."

"But who can tame the sea? If a woman is only a tributary to beauty, then one should seek an ample source such as an estuary where the river is widest. For my part, living with the court, surrounded by scores of beautiful women, is like constantly bathing in the most generous body of water."

"You cannot possibly understand my meaning," Michel said impatiently. "I have access to truths of which you have no conception. Do you recall the place at the roadside, when we were children?"

"Yes, you stood transfixed, looking into a tangle of watermarks in a mound of sandy earth. Once before when I asked what you saw, you refused to tell me."

"And now I shall. Were you standing there with me, you would have seen the wavering lines left behind by drying rainwater. Your sight would meld with the strange pattern in those alternating peaks and valleys, as perfect in their sequence as if a master engraver had left behind his noblest work. You would see many things, yet one: traces of rain in a field near our home, watermarks on the riverbanks of all the world; the sand of every ocean floor, every lake, stream, every body of water. You would know them all in an instant, and would promise yourself never, never to forget the vision entrusted to you."

The morning of Michel's wedding I woke very early with the knowledge special to such a day, a rite which not even the staunchest Reformer would dare deny.

I rose and restlessly walked the streets of Agen, finding that even in the early morning hours the marketplace bristled with brazen speakers who railed against

Pope and Church. When I found myself in their midst I recalled an incident of the previous year, one which even I (who usually considered myself distant to the religious disputes) had felt outraged by:

Boldly printed placards had appeared on that same day a year ago, had appeared on the very door of King François's bedchamber in the chateau of Blois. On the placards were words denouncing the clergy as vile filth, to use a euphemism. It was no wonder that the King vowed vengeance upon the placardists, and in his rage not only were scores of suspected printers arrested, but for a period of time all printing in France was banned.

In the first month of this year, the King announced his intention of making special amends, for the blasphemers remained unapprehended. An expiatory Mass was held in the Cathedral of Notre Dame. The King himself bore glowing tapers in each hand, carrying them as he walked gravely through the center of the grand nave along with his sons, his ambassadors and the nobles of the court. There before the altar he turned to the gathered crowd and swore allegiance to the Church, vowing to behead even his own children if ever they should be found in sympathy with the accursed heretics.

Now, hearing inflammatory words in the marketplace of Agen, I thought of the King's vow and hastened away from the crowds to avoid being mistaken for one of their followers. The sun was now higher in the sky, and it was time for me to return to Michel's home and to change into attire appropriate for the noontime ceremony.

Michel was handsomely fitted out, glowing with anticipation and much calmer than I would have been in the role of bridegroom. We walked together toward the Cathedral of Agen, where he paused before the doors and placed his hands on my shoulders.

"I am sparing with shows of emotion," he said softly, "but your presence here means more to me than I can say."

He then walked through the nave and took his place before the seated celebrants. The gilt altar flickered

with the glow of tallow candles as the bride and her
father appeared.

It was a cloudy day and though it seemed at first
that the sun would fail to release the colors of the leaded
glass windows, yet from overhead a determined shaft
of sunlight caught the glass and a rainbow of rose, gold,
emerald and indigo beamed down onto the couple kneel-
ing before the priest. Then as quickly as it had appeared, the sun disappeared behind clouds; the spectrum
faded, and the bride's flowing gown returned again to
the whiteness of marble.

My few days in Agen were over; the sacrament had
been bestowed. My friend Michel was now a married man,
a groom so filled with love for Madeleine that he bore little resemblance to the somber Michel I had known as a
child, or to the serious student of our university days. I
judged the transformation to be an improvement; it
seemed the nearest Michel had ever come to celebrating
life, an attitude he had often criticized in me.

I left Agen persuaded that Michel and I were finally
united in our natures. I also suspected this would not
hold true for long. No doubt love's transport would one
day weaken like a dying wind and Michel would be set
back on his old pathway toward gloomy goals. I hoped
it would not be soon.

He was only granted three years.

In those years, fortune looked graciously upon him:
two children were born, his wife bore them in good
health and skillfully tended their home. Michel's medical practice flourished and he looked ahead to a peaceful life among comrades, to quiet evenings at home with
his wife and children.

He wrote to me three times during the next nine
years, though perhaps other letters were sent and lost
since postal delivery depended upon the honoring of a
small payment to travelers heading for Paris.

In the first of those three letters he described his
happiness:

After supper each night I watch Madeleine as she
sits by the oil lamp near the hearth with her em-

broidery. Her needle glints in the firelight; she adds tiny, perfect stitches on the snowy cloth stretched tight in a wooden hoop on her lap. She holds her head at a thoughtful angle; one day this handiwork shall be worn as a communion dress for our second child.

Michel described how Madeleine would rise, folding the cloth over and over upon itself into a soft bundle; she would place it upon the chair, touching the back of her hand to her warm forehead, though Michel often cautioned her to sit farther from the hearth. As the hour grew late, she would kiss his cheek, then leave Michel alone to study until late into the night.

In those days he strolled the streets of Agen as a man above reproach, so highly regarded by the community that he feared no one, believed that no physician could ever again force his leave.

A year later, I heard from him again.

I write to inform you of the deepest sorrow of my life, the loss of my beloved wife and children. There have been many times during these four years in Agen when I have said to myself, "This is all a man could ever want," and yet I had the dread feeling that I had made a wrong turn, veering into another man's deserved place of peace. Now I know my premonition was true.

Despite his premonition, the sickness which claimed his family passed unnoticed until it was too late for Michel to help them. When Michel awoke one morning in the fourth year of his marriage, instead of finding his wife in her kitchen he noticed that she was still asleep, her body drenched with perspiration. Thinking it only a bad dream, he instructed the housekeeper to let her rest; he dressed quickly and set out for his daily rounds.

As Michel left his patient two hours later, he heard someone call his name and saw a young medical colleague standing across the road, waving frantically to capture Michel's attention.

"One of my patients has already succumbed to a sickness which confounds me," he said, his brow knit with perplexity. "You must come at once and give your opinion."

Michel protested that he was needed at home, to which the young man countered, "Nostradamus, you are a master of the healing arts so surely this disease will be no stranger to you. Think of the life you may save."

Reluctantly Michel followed him along a narrow street until they reached a small room where an entire family lay on rush mats in the close air of sickness.

"The old man worsens," the doctor whispered. "I saw his wife through this phase of the sickness yesterday and she did not live. I fear his end may be near. See how red his eyes are, and his tongue is swollen with a thick coating."

The man lay on his back with open eyes, staring vacantly at the smoke-stained ceiling.

"What can it be?" the doctor asked. "I have no way of treating this." He watched Michel expectantly, but Michel had no reply.

In another corner they examined a young woman whose thin face was flushed with fever, her bedclothes drenched with sweat.

"I know the symptoms," Michel said suddenly.

His colleague grasped Michel by the shoulders. "Then what is it—what shall we do for them?"

"I do not know. My wife was feverish and heavily perspiring when I left her hours ago. I must return home at once!" This time, the young doctor did not try to detain him. Michel ran from the fetid room and up the streets toward his home. Inside, the housekeeper stood over Madeleine, pressing a wet cloth to her forehead.

"She is worse," said the housekeeper. "Now her eyes are inflamed."

"I will prepare a medication," Michel said with false confidence, convincingly enough to assuage the fears of the housekeeper, whose wrinkled face managed a small, hopeful smile.

"Thank Our Lord you know exactly what to do, Doctor Nostradamus, for now the babies are feverish too."

Michel had no specific treatment to administer. The only thought in his mind was to remember that the old woman had died in one short day; he had but hours to devise some remedy for this mysterious sickness. If ever there was time when he needed composure to meditate upon a patient and prescribe the healing medication it was that day; yet fear for his own family rendered him nearly helpless. Though he entered the quiet storage room to gather his wits, to concentrate upon the problem, no answer came. The voice remained mute.

In desperation Michel applied every treatment that occurred to him in a great confusion of compresses and herbal concoctions, with hot bricks to sweat out the illness, then, in a change of mind, cool cloths to reduce the fever.

The housekeeper never once questioned Michel's contradictory methods or the endless cups of liquid which he spooned between his wife's lips. With complete faith, the old woman aided him, thinking these methods time-tested and sure.

"Nostradamus," the young doctor called, pounding on the door. "Come with me at once—I must have your help!"

The housekeeper opened the door; the doctor saw Madeleine. "My God," he swore softly, "even the great doctor has no cure."

Michel shook his head. The housekeeper saw this exchange and stopped in her tracks; a wet cloth just removed from Madeleine's forehead hung limp in her hand. On her face was neither sympathy nor concern; she recoiled from the sight of the sick woman in horror and stared at Nostradamus as though he were a demonic impostor.

The sun had long since set; in the candlelight grotesque shadows danced on Madeleine's damp skin. Steam rose from an herbal medication simmering on the flames, and the cries of Michel's children tormented him nearly to madness. His eyes met the housekeeper's and he saw her unspoken condemnation. He could bear it no longer.

"If you are concerned for their recovery, then go to the church and pray. Pray for yourself too; you can do no good here." Silently she drew on a wrap and departed.

Alone with his family in the flickering light, faint from exhaustion, Michel rested for a moment and in that brief time he thought of other nights like this when first he became a physician. In that past time, though the strange sights and sounds were terrifying, yet they held a certain fascination; then he faced a young man's battle, and his victory was sweet. When he achieved an almost saintly fame, the cries and pain became justifications for his life, dire illness the guarantee of his good name; but now, in the mirror of infirmity around him, Nostradamus saw his family near death, himself whole and soon to be alone. The inner voice was silent as never before.

Just before daybreak, Michel removed two of the heavy quilts from Madeleine's bed. She remained unconscious. The fever and thrashing were past, and in their passing faded the illusion of struggle for life as she lay still in Michel's arms.

He walked in the funeral procession behind the three biers, barely aware of the accusing stares of his townsmen. In his grief, he heard some voices retelling how he had saved many lives, but the rest looked coldly upon the great doctor, condemning his fallibility.

The people of Agen had not known Michel's work during the plague years, but only knew of his fame, his past laurels. To them, he was a miracle worker. Surely, he had remedies for their everyday complaints, but now that the city was stricken by some nameless pestilence he was unable to dignify his name. He refused them miracles in a time when faith—like friendship, always fragile—crumbled throughout France. For this, they cursed him.

Michel's beloved home turned ugly before his aggrieved eyes. In only a few weeks his wife's family had raised suit to reclaim her dowry. Even Scaliger turned away from him, for to César, Michel's presence was a reminder of his error in judgment in choosing this man as his protégé, colleague, friend. Even with Scaliger's rejection, Michel stubbornly remained in Agen, determined not to be expelled from his home again.

Michel's practice dwindled to a few loyal patients and Madeleine's dowry was awarded to her family. Michel's home and furnishings were sold to restore to his in-laws the original dowry in silver. After this disheartening litigation was done, Michel found himself in modest rented lodgings. There he remained for over a year, turning to his studies of astrology and ancient symbols as consolation in his loneliness.

In 1538 he again wrote, saying,

I shall soon be departing from Agen, surrendering another home to my persecutors. Although I believed I had reached the depths of suffering, and had convinced myself that through a terrible penance I would emerge a humbler man, I have recently faced an adversary who brought me nearer to execution than any plague.

It began with a small incident in January of the preceding year. Michel was walking past the workshop of a metal craftsman; he looked inside and saw the craftsman's finished work strewn randomly along a dirty and cluttered wooden shelf: a dozen bronze images of the Virgin irreverently heaped among shrunken bits of cheese and rat droppings. Enraged by the blasphemy, Michel barged into the shop. The hem of his woolen robe swept through scraps of metal and refuse on the dirty floor. Confronting the bewildered craftsman he pointed to the statues and cried, "You degrade the Virgin as though she were some unwashed whore."

"My man, mind your tongue," cautioned a neighbor who had stopped in the doorway. Restraining Michel, the man led him away from the workshop. In the cool air outside the shop, Michel dimly understood the warning words: "The court of the Inquisition has ears behind walls, in the streets, in the most hidden of places."

A fortnight later a knock on his door brought Michel to hopeful alertness, since he rarely had visitors. But when he opened the door, Michel found himself facing an official who addressed him sourly, "Michel de Nostredame, called Nostradamus?"

"I am he."

"I carry a warrant for your arrest. You are to appear before the Court of the Inquisition in Toulouse."

"I am charged with heresy?" Michel was dumbfounded.

"This should be no surprise to you. Two witnesses have testified, a craftsman and his assistant. You have until the sand in this hourglass has run half its course," he said, turning the glass on Michel's small bedside table.

Michel wrote a brief note to Scaliger in those few minutes remaining to him, begging Scaliger for help in his perilous situation, but he held out little hope of a reply.

For seven days, Michel waited within a stinking cell in Toulouse; at night he slept cramped in a miserable position on the cold floor. Finally one morning he was taken from the cell to an anteroom where he waited with a dozen of the accused until their names were called to enter the judgment chamber.

When at last Michel was summoned, he followed upon a group of rag-tag young men who were being led away from the bench. They were tied together at their waists by a connecting length of rope with its free end wrapped around the wrist of a dour old guard.

Michel knelt before the court and averted his eyes from those who held him in judgment. A lengthy detailing of statutes preceded the statement of Michel's alleged crime. While the bailiff droned on, Michel carefully raised his eyes and considered those who would determine his future. Seated before him at a small, ornate table was the scribe, his head a hairless dome, his mouth framed by parentheses of grim lines. The first joint of his finger marked Michel's case in the thick book of records half-buried beneath his voluminous sleeves.

Behind the scribe on a raised dais draped with velvet sat the high official, dozing on his throne of judgment. His napping gave a misleading atmosphere of laxity and indifference, but Michel was not consoled, nor did he expect leniency from the four Churchmen who sat behind the official. Their icy faces signaled that they would end his life with no pang of conscience on a burning pyre.

Of the men, one stared at Michel with such concentration that Michel believed his judgment was already sealed.

Finally, the bailiff's voice changed to an audible pitch as he enumerated the specific charges against Michel:

"You are summoned to this Court to face the following charge: On January 2, 1537, you the accused, Michel de Nostredame, did blaspheme the name of the Holy Virgin. This blasphemy did occur within the foundry of Henri Montcoeur, bronzesmith. In that place and on that day, the accused did point to statues of the Holy Virgin which were being prepared for use of the Church; there, witnesses testify that M. Nostredame did curse the statues, calling the Virgin 'an unwashed whore.'"

"How do you plead to these charges?" asked the judge, who had roused himself from sleep.

"Those were my words but my intention was not to blaspheme the Virgin," Michel replied. "The Holy Mother has long been represented by such statues to aid the faithful in knowing her beauty of spirit by seeing beauty in a visible form—but when I saw the same statues piled in leavings and ordure, I could not bear the thought of Her Holiness being so debased. The bronzesmith who testified against me is your heretic; he should have no hand in the manufacture of sacred objects."

"Your explanation does not exonerate you of the charge of blasphemy," said the official. "According to my records, you are the same Nostradamus who resided in Narbonne during the pestilence of 1525, only to be driven from that city for practicing the black arts. It is also noted that you engaged in unorthodox medical practices in Toulouse during 1528."

"Are you he?" asked the cleric who had been impaling Michel with his stare.

"I am," Michel replied, all hope lost.

"Then I entreat you, my respected fellow jurors, to accept this man's defense and decide upon acquittal, for by his powers as healer, and by the administration of a lozenge which God granted him the knowledge to prescribe, this man did many years ago in Toulouse preserve my life."

When the Court of the Inquisition finally acquitted Michel, the restored freedom to return to his barren existence seemed scarcely more beneficent than the finality of flames. He returned to Agen, packed a few belongings and, with a handful of coins hidden in the lining of a riding cloak, he traveled northward as if a new direction would rectify his life. Once again Michel found himself among the faithful, the adventurous, and the displaced as he traveled the roadways of France.

One night at an inn near Limoges, one of the pilgrims in whose company he found himself that evening mistakenly took him for one of their own and inquired of Michel, "Which shrine is your destination?" to which Michel simply replied, "I will know when I see the shrine before me."

Thus began the most significant of Michel's travels. I did not hear from him until another five years were to pass; until then I had no idea of his whereabouts and only knew that he had departed from Agen. Yet I never doubted that we would see each other again.

When he wrote me later, I learned that his journey began that night with the innocent words Michel spoke about pilgrimage, for the three pilgrims in the Limoges inn took his remark as impertinence; offended, they moved their plates to the farthest end of the long table, and thus cleared the way for an exchange which would lead Michel on the very pilgrimage he hoped for.

"Pardon me," said a jovial man who sat across the way. "I overheard your conversation and I must compliment you on your reply. You speak like a philosopher." He now seated himself, uninvited, beside Michel. He was a stocky man some years older than Nostradamus, and he held a thick joint of mutton in his hand. "Possibly you are a hedonist, like myself," he said, proceeding to bite off a strip of meat from the lamb bone. A glistening stream of juice ran from the corner of his mouth.

"I am neither holy man nor hedonist," Michel replied. "I am without feeling, beyond the consolation of faith or pleasure."

"No, no, my good man, pleasure is precisely what one needs in desperate times, for though you may not know it, pleasure begets pleasure and eventually one is happy in spite of himself."

The stranger's enthusiasm was irresistible; he had captured Michel's curiosity.

"I see you are a man of intelligence," said the stocky man. "This is a rare treat for a constant traveler like myself, for usually I am surrounded by contentious traders, brigands and tedious pilgrims. Tell me, what really *is* your destination?"

"Truly I have none."

Michel's answer further delighted him; he interpreted it not as indifference toward the future but, as he himself would intend such a reply, as a willingness to follow any beckoning path.

"I do not wish to pry into your affairs, but if you are continuing north on this road tomorrow, then you will pass near a thermal station. I think I shall stop there, for perhaps a week, in order to rest before traveling on to Paris. I have an obligation to my body: I must care for it well, lest ill health should restrict my pleasure. Perhaps you would care to join me?"

Michel followed an impulse and answered, "Yes, I would not mind a few days' rest, though a water cure is no remedy for my distress."

"Nonetheless, you will benefit from it—and you will enjoy the delectable food! But let us introduce ourselves: I am Etienne DuPere," he said.

Michel gave his name and saw, with relief, that DuPere had never heard of him.

* * *

They departed from the inn early next morning in a thick mist. By late afternoon, when they ascended a knoll, the thermal station appeared as columns of smoke rising from the chimneys of half-timbered buildings. DuPere and Nostradamus led their mounts into a compound arranged around the central baths like walls of a small fortress.

"Which inn do you recommend?" Michel asked. There were several, each with a colorful hanging emblem denoting the name of the inn for the benefit of the unlettered. Among them were the Fleur de Lis, the Black Doe, the Copper Bell and the Blue Halberd.

"I lodge at the Black Doe," said DuPere as he gave his mule to a groom, nodding at Michel to relinquish his. Michel could smell the sulphuric brown water as it gurgled forth from subterranean depths and sent a low-lying veil of steam into the cool afternoon air.

The sun had disappeared behind the brick and timbered inn; the baths were now empty. The stone steps on each end that led into the rectangular pool were wide and shallow, easy to climb for the elderly and infirm who flocked to the baths each year. An uneven border of wooden planks was propped around the hot pool and slanted down to the edge of the water. It served as a simple shelter for the bathers, who would stand beneath the lean-to as a respite from sun and peering eyes.

Michel and DuPere were led to their rooms. Michel slept soundly, although he woke twice and in his groggy state of half-sleep he thought the acrid smell was some medication, a poultice, an astringent herb.

He woke to the sound of bathers entering their baths; he heard loud voices and displaced water lapping against stone walls. Michel glanced from his window and saw that what had appeared as murky brown water the night before was now clear and sparkling in the sunlight. From his second-story room, the pool appeared to have caught the reflection of a single lime tree on the south end of the rectangle, its shimmering likeness as an image in rippled glass.

In minutes he was down the stairs, leaving Etienne DuPere snoring across the hall in his bed. Michel stood at the edge of the pool and saw a steady stream of pure water feeding from a trough by the lime tree into the pool. A dozen ceramic cups were provided for drinking. As he surveyed the thermal baths he forgot the promised breakfast of fried bread and broth, and instead was drawn to the wooden trough with its outpouring of water, for he knew it flowed from a pure place within the earth. Grasping a cup, submerging it in the trough, he began to administer to his own malady.

He walked past a line of sycamore canes propped against the wall, provided for the aid of elderly bathers; then he found an empty shelter, ducked beneath it and somewhat reluctantly removed his tunic, hose and shoes before he sank into the pool. Immersed in warm water, his taut muscles loosened, and within a few minutes his body felt lighter, his limbs loose and flexible. The ingested water filled his stomach while the pool bathed his skin. Michel was one of the younger bathers. Around him in the swirling waters, making waves or rivulets with their movements, a score of elderly men and a few women were submerged in steaming water up to their fleshy chins.

At midday Michel retreated from the sun and sought the shade of a wooden shelter. Finding one unoccupied, he had just leaned back against the stone wall and was listening to the water lapping about his ears when a vendor walked by.

"Apples," he cried. "Buy my sweet fruit and hasten your cure."

Michel peered over the wall just as a basket full of bright red apples passed by. He was about to call for one when from the shelter adjacent to his own a scratchy voice called out.

"Take my advice: fast and take only water the first day. Tomorrow add a piece of fruit, then after the second day you may follow your appetite, though in moderation."

"Surely you are not a physician," Michel said, chagrined at the audacity of a layman offering him advice.

"No, but I have resided here for nearly a year," said the old man. "On Saint Andrew's Day last, my family gave me up as a dying man. Do I look it now? No, but first I had to convince them to bring me here and then in desperation I listened to anyone who offered advice. Now, a year later, I am grateful to the baths and to those who spoke truly; in good faith, I offer my knowledge to you."

Admitting that this man did not now, if once he had, resemble a dying man, Michel asked, "Why did you choose this place?"

"A year ago a dear friend insisted that I travel to Lorraine, where he arranged a consultation with a fortuneteller. I had always sworn I'd never bother with soothsayers, but my friend insisted—and so I went. In the presence of this gifted man, I realized that the others I had known were charlatans. His words were veiled and odd, but I had trust in him from the first meeting, and it was by his direction that I came here."

"Then this fortuneteller told you to come?"

"Not directly. Here is how it was: I remained in his home three days. His wife gave me light food and I was treated gently. He spoke to me in a soft, rhythmic voice about stars and planets, of a sacred alphabet, of colors and geometrical shapes and the interrelationship of these became as clear as if I had always known. For three days I listened and slept and dreamed unusual dreams. Then on the fourth day, an answer occurred to me as a voice within myself. But it spoke in the manner of the fortuneteller himself, and I knew the words were true. On the fifth day I thanked this man for his help, and I began the journey here."

Michel lay in the warm waters, breathing deeply of its vapors and wondering at the fulcrum of words and their power to lead a man all the way to these thermal baths from Lorraine—only to propel Michel in the same direction; now he knew where his pilgrimage would lead. He looked at the serene old man bathing next to him. A dusty road and a fortnight of country hostels separated Michel's future and the old man's past.

"I shall leave tomorrow," Michel informed Etienne that evening as they sat in the Black Doe together, Michel with a mug of spring water in his hand, Etienne with a heaping platter of roast pork. Michel did not explain, nor did Etienne demand an explanation; Etienne only sighed, the sigh of a man who judged his companion a fool for leaving the comfort of the thermal station after only one day and, unforgivably, without even partaking of a meal at the highly acclaimed board of the Black Doe. But Michel's appetite was only for an immediate departure; the slabs of pork swimming in rich brown gravy would be an impossible burden for a body readied for flight.

Michel's pilgrimage began the following morning; in place of a sacred token, he carried a slip of paper with the name of the fortuneteller, Thières, and the street on which he kept lodgings.

Once again traveling purposefully, Michel regained much of his lost faculty for concentration and by the time he arrived at Thières's home, Michel's mind was more lucid than it had been in many months, his judgment in day-to-day matters almost as keen as before his wife's death.

"I have been expecting you," Thières said, as a servant took Michel's riding cloak and bags. Thières led him through a modest parlor and down a narrow stone stair to a subterranean room.

"You have studied the Mysteries before," Thières said. "My task will be smoother as you are a man of understanding...though I perceive that you have lost the Sight from time to time. Tell me of your teachers."

"My grandfather told me of secret matters," Michel said, "but he died when I was a boy. Except for fragments of his teachings and the memory of a vision I saw as a child, I consider myself a man of small understanding. I do have a grasp of the principles of astrology, which I learned in Avignon years ago."

The room was sparsely furnished, only a few feet in width from cellar wall to cellar wall, and Michel felt as though he were in a grotto. Thières spread a pack of cards upon a stone table.

"Your token is the cup," Thières said when the cards were arranged before them. "It embodies the receptive imagination, and yours is of such capacity that all time shall flow before your eyes. You shall give it form before the world."

"Your words disturb me. What does this mean?"

"You possess a gift which was revealed earlier in your life, is this not true?"

"Perhaps, when I first became a physician. During the reign of *le charbon* I discovered this gift; it came to me as a faculty for seeing causes and cures. But that was many years ago."

"The gift lies hidden. Through discipline you must learn to control this vision of the flow of time which will be revealed to you, in order to accomplish your great work for mankind."

"What discipline will direct my course?"

"A secret language of signs and numbers which mirror all creation. Life can be told in its terms."

"Will you accept me as your student?" asked Michel. "I cannot pay a large fee because my recent period of trial has left me with only a few coins and a change of clothing. But I am not without resources; I am a doctor trained in Montpellier, and in time I could repay you."

"Do not talk of payment. It is my obligation to teach the qualified pupil when he presents himself to me. I cannot shirk this responsibility and yet retain my power. Even were I to charge you, the debt would be small, for you shall not be in Lorraine six months from this day."

"You misunderstand. I have every intention of remaining until I have mastered the knowledge."

"You may intend to remain here. Your decision is founded on a desire to study the Mysteries and as yet you see with shortsighted eyes. I am the only teacher you see; my eyes are of a man who stands on a hill and views the horizon of your future: I see other teachers who will follow me."

"How do you see my future?"

"I cannot see your time in clear detail. Some events are faint possibilities while others are sharply formed as you advance toward them. The latter are strong tendencies and I would call them inevitable. Today I tell you of this process; you will understand fully someday."

"So you tell me I shall see the future and share my vision with mankind. But I do not desire to do this—I do not want the curse of Jeremiah, to foresee the future and find myself despised or thought a fool."

Thières smiled kindly and his voice was sad as he said, "It is not for *you* to choose."

Michel remained in Lorraine four months and during that time, under the guidance of Thières, he studied a complex system of correspondences. In one exercise he was to focus attention upon the internal links between colors of the spectrum and the ancient pictorial forms of the Hebrew alphabet.

One night Michel patiently gazed at a candle by his bedside. His course of study that night concerned the letter Tzaddi, the fish and hook, in its correspondence with the color violet.

Hours passed. Michel fought the urge to curl up on his bed and sink into a deserved sleep; then the drowsiness passed and he entered a new realm, the wisdom of night beyond dreaming.

The white light of the candle shattered suddenly into a rainbow arc around the flame. Thières had cautioned Michel not to interrupt his concentration on the gold-white flame for any reason, yet at the moment of this appearance Michel strained his eyes to catch a glimpse of the violet band of light lurking at the edge of his vision.

He tried to encompass the outer ring, but the intense central flame burned into his eyes. The pain bore deep into his sockets. Then a veil seemed to fall, a trance; he sank beneath the flame as though dropping a line into the depths of a molten sea... and many fathoms below he saw Tzaddi as the fish which dwells beneath the sea of awakening and as the hook which brings hidden life from shadows into light. There he glimpsed an order secluded in dark chaos.

Throughout the months with Thières, Michel learned of the transparent threads which weave all living fragments into unity. Thières would not allow Michel to labor, for he explained that this new manner of thinking was unlike the practical logic necessary for everyday decisions, those lines of reasoning which link like kinds. His discipline was to understand the linking of what the common world saw as dissimilar. Michel was trained to cut across everyday categories until, unhampered by limitations, his mind would flow from subject to subject, following only the internal language and logic of secret symbols.

"You will have to return to the practical world soon enough," said Thières, "and when you do, in practical matters you shall be even wiser than before."

Though Michel was intrigued by this adventure of the spirit, nonetheless in four months he became unaccountably restless, barely able to hold his mind on a subject for longer than moments. When Michel confessed this problem to Thières, fully expecting his teacher to chastise him for lack of dedication, Thières merely replied: "I expected you to encounter this obstacle, and now that you have come against it, I am no longer your teacher."

"Why did you accept me as a student, if you knew of this limitation?"

"I accepted you because I had a portion of truth to offer. But no final answers, no peace of mind."

Michel turned to the road again and searched the faces of fellow travelers for a sign. Would this man, or that, lead him in the right direction? He sought the company of those who bore resemblance to Thières, to his grandfather, to LeCler, hoping that like qualities could be found thereby. And yet when the sign appeared after weeks of traveling southward again, Michel almost tossed it away.

It was late in the afternoon of a dark, rainy day near Avignon. The proximity to the city where he had lived for two years as a hopeful student caused Michel to feel old and disillusioned. He sat with a half-dozen other lodgers at the Inn of the Red Dog, passing the afternoon with mulled wine and conversation as each traveler told a tale more exaggerated than the last.

"To be in Venice on a rainy day such as this..." said a man who had not bothered to remove his mud-spattered shoes. The others sat forward attentively as all caught a whiff of another ribald story in the making.

"When I was in Venice, I'd watch the rain pour onto the piazza of San Marco. And when the rain stopped, I would sail along the Grand Canal until I reached the home of beautiful Raphaella."

"Ah," the men sighed, encouraging the storyteller to spare no detail.

"I'd light on her waterfront doorway with an armful of gladioli to prepare the way for the mood of love." He paused with a frown, prompting one man among the rapt listeners to urge, "What happened next, pray tell?"

"Unfortunately," he shrugged, "as soon as I dream of that delicious girl, I am repulsed by the thought of her father. I call him a charlatan, and yet he had a moneyed following who sought his advice and called him 'the oracle of the Adriatic.' His stinking pigeons! He had the gall to claim he could read my 'ignoble future' in their droppings, or some such nonsense."

This prophet of Venice intrigued Michel, and he pondered a way to glean more information without rousing the storyteller's jealousy.

"You are a fine teller of tales," Michel said, shaking the man's hand. "Such eloquence and perception!"

This gesture assured Michel that for the remainder of the evening he would be engaged with the man in the muddy boots, though the result was not the slightest piece of useful news. He must find his direction another way; with the hook of understanding. Resolved, the next morning he began his quest.

Throughout the southward trip to Italy it seemed that the rain would never cease, nor would Michel's boots ever again be dry. Yet after three weeks of sleet and unmerciful showers, Michel finally reached the fabled city. At a distance her domes and spires rose from a lavender mist, and as Michel looked across a canal dotted by small craft, he saw the magnificent piazza with its scattering of pigeons. He walked the narrow alleyways and squandered coins on gondoliers who only brought him back to where he had begun.

Somewhere in the grand city dwelt a man who read future time in the flight of birds. Though he had no information, and though none of the strangers he asked was able to offer a clue, yet Michel believed a lost object could be found by another device. With this purpose,

he first took a room for the night; once inside it he
began an exercise in concentration to clarify his mind
and to focus upon the problem. He repeated the question
over and over again: "Somewhere in this city is a man
who reads the flight of birds. How am I to find him?"

In the candle flame on his bedstand, darting images
began to appear, images from memory, fragments of
conversation ... "cages of pigeons" ... "a doorway on the
Grand Canal".... Impressions of his first day in Venice
rose and faded in the rainbow-arc around the flame:
grand and humble buildings, bridges large and small,
wide canals and narrow watery passageways.

Michel could hold his eyes open no longer. He extinguished the candle and lay fully clothed atop his bed,
hoping to rest only a few moments, but instead he slipped
into a deep sleep.

He dreamed of the spires of Venice and of soft rustling wings that grew to a thunderous sound; he saw
clouds of birds circling the domes of San Marco a short
distance away. They rested on the tops of columns and
their sound diminished to a soft rustling once more; the
image shrank to a single rooftop with crenellated walls
and a small round window overlooking a winding canal.
The angle of light indicated midmorning as easterly
sunlight rose in the sky behind him. Among the myriad
rooftops, behind the wall, stood a man with his young
assistant, flushing the pigeons back into their cages.

The following morning Michel woke stiff with chill
from an open window. The sun was already rising higher
in the sky, approaching the hour seen in his dream.
Michel hastened down the stairs of the lodging house,
and his destination was as clear as a page of written
directions.

He walked with the sun at his back toward the Grand
Canal, but when he approached a familiar bridge and
crossed, he stopped suddenly, uncertain of which course
to choose. It seemed his map had been withdrawn
abruptly.

Then from above Michel heard the beating of wings;
over his head a cloud of pigeons rose from a house behind a crenellated wall. Seeing his dream in daylight,

Michel reeled with faintness and leaned for support
upon a nearby gate. When he felt his strength return,
he approached the door of the house and struck its lion-
head clapper.

"Signor Giolo is not accepting visitors," said the servant curtly.

"Who is there?" Michel heard a woman's voice from
inside.

"Tell the lady I am Doctor Nostradamus of Saint-
Rémy in Provence, and that I have journeyed far to
consult with Signor Giolo. I know he is here, for only
a moment ago I heard his pigeons on the roof and they
were not enclosed in their cages."

"There are thousands of pigeons in Venice," said the
woman, who emerged from another room and approached Michel in the doorway, curious no doubt to
see this insistent visitor.

Indeed she was lovely. Michel at once decided that
the traveler at the Red Dog Inn was unworthy to touch
even the hem of her silken gown. As he stood before
Raphaella, Michel felt a surge of confidence, adventurer
once more. "I must see your father," Michel stated.

"I will take you to him, then," said the young woman,
her appraising look turning now to an amused smile.
But Michel's audience began on a discouraging note.

"I am too old to accept another pupil, Nostradamus,"
Giolo sighed, as though weary of answering such questions. Michel wondered if perhaps he was merely one
in a line of eager students who had sat in this study,
only to be refused.

"I only disclose my secrets to the apprentice who has
served me for a dozen years," he said slowly as he scru-
tinize ' Michel, who showed little willingness to leave.
"But, Giolo continued, "I believe you are sincere. Since
you have traveled far, let me extend this offer: stay as
my guest for a fortnight; observe us at our work and
feel at liberty to ask any questions."

"A generous offer, Master Giolo," Michel said. "I shall
remain—and you may expect *many* questions."

Michel followed Giolo to the rooftop where hundreds
of pigeons were clustered in cages, nibbling their corn

and meal, clucking and cooing behind wooden slats. He waited quietly as the master prepared to divine the answer to a nobleman's query.

The inquiry concerned the fate of the man's son, who had departed for India six months earlier on a trading expedition. During that time there had been no word. Was the young man alive? Was he alive, but ill? Was he being held captive?

Giolo's assistant carried a chair onto the roof terrace and placed it in a designated area marked by a painted design. The master seated himself, touched his fingers to his eyelids, muttered words which Michel could not understand.

Several minutes passed. At last Giolo nodded to the assistant, who tossed two handfuls of corn onto the roof then raised the slatted door of a large cage, releasing dozens of the pigeons who swarmed about the corn, puffing up their feathers and bobbing their heads after the bright kernels.

Michel watched Giolo, who appeared to be staring at the birds, his eyes glassy, lids partly closed.

Suddenly the scene changed. In a movement which the assistant made without any discernible sign from his master, the young man clapped his hands sharply twice; the pigeons rose from the ground in a startled gray mass.

Giolo lurched forward in his chair, raised his head as the flock of pigeons soared upward and scattered across the morning sky. Giolo's lips began to tremble; he spoke inaudibly. The assistant rushed to his side and inscribed notes on a small tablet.

After recording Giolo's vision, the man helped his master from the chair and led him down the narrow staircase into the study. Michel was told by Raphaella that now Giolo would rest, but that he would be willing to discuss the oracle with Michel later that afternoon.

Michel waited impatiently until the servants had removed the remnants of the afternoon meal. "Master Giolo," he said, "may I ask what you saw this morning?"

"Among creatures in flight, in their frantic confusion, I also saw a dark young man in anguish, near death, and so far away that I knew he would never return to his home."

"Did you see this man distinctly—does no doubt remain in your mind?" Michel probed the old man, remembering a remark of Thières that some images are clear while others are obscure and visible only as vague shapes.

"Of course I saw the young man clearly. I am never mistaken."

"Master Giolo, why do you foretell the future by observing birds' flight?" Michel's question had the effect he intended, for Giolo was fond of recounting his own tales of spiritual education.

"When I was a young man and first set forth to find my teacher, just as you seek a teacher today, I knew when I saw my master's flock that this secret way would open to me if only I followed the same path. Though it required many long and discouraging years to perfect the art, perfect it I have."

"You were fortunate to be so single-minded," Michel said, "for I seem to face nothing but confusion after sitting at the feet of four teachers."

"You may find your voice and your vision one day, Nostradamus. Some do, many fail. Perhaps it would benefit your studies to visit an acquaintance of mine. It is a long journey to Sicily, but you have traveled far already, and what is a few leagues more? And the weather is temperate farther south at this time of year."

"Does he read the flight of birds?"

"No, he reads the message of fire, or what he calls its whisperings, the message of smoke. He is younger than I, and may be willing to instruct such an eager student," Giolo said, pressing his recommendation. Michel suspected this was an effort to dispatch him as soon as possible, rather than allow a young man to remain under the same roof as his beautiful daughter.

"The Sicilian may be a hermit, but I urge that you seek him out. When you near the village of Adrano, I am sure any stranger can show you the way." He closed his eyes, as if summoning a vision, then added, "Yes, I see that Sicily will be the crucial point of all your travels."

It was, all told, a brief stay in Venice for Michel, and only four days after his arrival he departed for Calabria, then across the straits of Messina to Adrano, at the foot of Mount Etna. With no difficulty he found the abode of the hermit, who spoke little yet accepted Michel as his student. It was a wordless apprenticeship, and at first the man who called himself Barra seemed an incarnation of the fiery spirit he summoned from the embers, so florid was his face and red his beard. But contrary to Michel's first impression, his teacher withheld no book and concealed no gesture. By silent observation, Michel furthered his art.

After two months had passed, Barra motioned for Michel to enter the cluttered chamber he called his sanctum. The last rays of sun had set behind the mountain.

Michel sat on a rough bench in the corner of the room. He watched Barra drape a faded black cape across his shoulders, as if immersing himself in ashes. He then sprinkled drops of pungent oil into the brass bowl atop a tripod. Small twigs and bark gathered that morning were placed in the brazier, and with a touch of a taper his work began.

The flame grew like fingers of a hand, spreading from the brass bowl; from the fingertips wisps of smoke curled upward to the low ceiling.

As his eyes followed the smoke, Michel posed a question: "What will become of me? Will I wander until I die, ever denied wisdom?"

From the smoke came a murmur of sound, a promise of understanding. Nostradamus saw himself in a strange room where he stood beside another tripod, gazing from an upper window that overlooked a lovely town surrounded with green fields. The buildings and shops of the town were clear; he had passed this way during his early years of wandering. But if this was the same town he remembered, it was surrounded not by lush greenery but by arid, thirsty soil.

Michel had seen his future. After countless inns and villages and byways, he knew the pathway home. Giolo had been right: Sicily was the point of his return.

* * *

Michel's destiny unfolded before him like the script on a parchment scroll. It began thus: on the third day, traveling from Adrano on a dusty road between Randazzo and Taormina, a man approached Michel from the north. He traveled alone, and Michel thought this surprising, for both travelers risked injury by journeying without companions on such dangerous roads.

As the man neared, Michel recognized the brown robe of a monastic order. Though he could not see the man's face from such a distance, he knew by his bearing that this was a youth of ambitious nature. Fascinated by the power of the monk's energetic stride, Michel lapsed into a reverie. With the approaching footsteps, the stranger's body dissolved into waves of motion; he melted before Nostradamus's eyes into fluid shapes and colors, from formless gray into purest white, then into crimson. Before him, Michel saw an older man—a man dressed in papal robes; on his hand the ring of Saint Peter dazzled Michel's eyes.

"Your Holiness," Michel cried, prostrating himself at the monk's feet.

The young monk did not push Nostradamus aside nor denounce him as a madman. When Michel raised his head and looked into the stranger's eyes, he saw within them an understanding: this man knew his own destiny as surely as Michel recognized it.

Michel set forth again in a northwesterly direction, urged on by the verdant town he had envisioned in the curling smoke. But before he was to secure the home of his imagining, further challenges barred his way.

The six-month sojourn in Italy spared him from knowledge of a pestilence incurred by a long and sopping springtime, but as he again walked on French soil a squall assailed him and he sought refuge in a country manor with vine-covered walls.

Michel struck his fists upon the heavy door, unaware that any purpose other than shelter could be served. A servant first appeared, then a portly man who filled the doorframe with his blue-robed girth. He wore an extravagantly full beard equal to his stature.

"I am Michel de Nostredame, of Saint-Rémy, a physician and traveler who now returns to his home after many months abroad."

"And at this moment you are wet and cold from this unrelenting rain," said the man, whose name was de Florinville.

"This is true, and I would appreciate a cup of water—perhaps a while before your hearth."

"A small request. I am honored," said de Florinville, shaking his head at the persistent downpour. "It is rare to have so distinguished a visitor as Doctor Nostradamus; indeed it is my pleasure to offer you hospitality."

Michel removed his cloak and sat before the warming fire, placing his boots as near the flames as leather would allow.

Within an hour the rain subsided, although briefly, and while Michel would have preferred to remain inside, the squire insisted on a tour around his property.

"I have heard of your potions and talismans, Nostradamus. Now if you are a magician, as some say, then tell me this: on which of these piglets shall we dine? Surely it is in your power to read the future."

A few steps away, in the pigsty, the squire's two sons were sliding about in the muck, in pursuit of a porker for the afternoon meal.

"It shall be the black one," Michel said, just as the squire's eldest son held up his catch, a squeaking white pig with brown spots; its body jerked desperately as it dangled from the boy's dirty hands.

"Ha—Doctor, your prediction may yet come true. We may have the black piglet for supper—say, *next* week." The man rubbed his hands together gleefully. "Of course, I asked you which was to be eaten tonight. Or did I specify? Will you defend your answer by saying I phrased the question too loosely and therefore your answer could prove true at some future time?"

"No, sir, I fully understood your question, and my answer remains thus: we shall dine this very day upon only the black pig."

"Come, come, you are stubborn, Nostradamus. But don't let this business of predicting come between us, for I enjoy your company. Tell me of your travels and tell me of Italy! Did you visit the Eternal City?" he asked, placing his arm again around Michel's shoulder.

No more was said of the piglet that afternoon.

But at table, come evening, the entire family of seven was seated around the heavily laden board, all staring at their distinguished guest.

Festive country dishes brimmed with home-grown fare, set out so generously there was barely room for the plates. Yet an empty space remained in the center of the table for the roast pig, soon to be served.

Wine was poured into five shining cups, a hearty red vintage produced on the manor grounds and enjoyed by all but the younger children.

"Ah—our sweet spotted pig," the squire announced when the cook appeared with a covered platter and set it among the bright dishes of food.

The squire removed the cover then drew in his breath, dropping the lid into a dish of simmered tomatoes and causing the contents to splash across the linen cloth in a wave of red sauce. There on the glazed platter, with an apple in its mouth, lay the black piglet.

"Charles!" cried the host, "where is the spotted beast you caught this morning?"

"I hit it on the head, Father, and set it on the slab to run its blood, as you have told me to do."

"But a milkmaid walked past and he followed her into the stable," interrupted the younger boy. "And I followed along to see what they would do."

The boy's mother cut short the details.

"Well, a wolf carried off the spotted piglet," said the eldest boy, red-faced, "so we had to catch another."

The red stain seeped into the linen cloth.

"I shall have to swallow my skepticism, along with a bit of this predestined pig," said the squire, as he began to carve the roast. "I compliment you, Doctor Nostradamus. Indeed, you are no charlatan, though it may be an exaggeration to compare this incident with the prophecies of Biblical times. Yes, I have witnessed—but exactly what have I seen? This is the difficulty you face, for even if others believe you it remains that in our time it is dangerous to be thought in league with the devil. Of course, we know you are a Christian man and not a false prophet, but a healer."

"Yes, these are times of pestilence," Michel said, to shift the subject. "Perhaps you are right, Squire. I am needed where sickness is severe and I have decided to depart tomorrow for Marseilles. Of course, you have been most instrumental in my decision."

"I thank God for my small part," he replied, making the sign of the cross upon his breast. "To think I might indirectly help those poor souls."

"Otherwise it might spread to us here," his wife added.

On the road to Marseilles, Michel traveled through ruined fields and beside rivers swollen with corpses of animals, fragments of wood that once were part of a barn, a shed, a home. The foul stench rising from the river prompted him to gather handfuls of pungent wild greens; he inhaled the scent, and his distress lessened.

Throughout the south of France the foul rivers dispensed a pestilence. Worst of all plague cities was Aix, where the sickness had begun the previous May. By the time of Michel's arrival, the place had become a phantom site of abandoned buildings, its streets wildly grown over with weeds for lack of treading feet. Cobblestones lay about in disrepair; potholes were filled with filth.

So absolute was the despair of the people of Aix that once stricken, the victims would abandon all hope of recovery and would wrap themselves for death in two white winding sheets. This most gruesome of plague cities reeked from its dead, its wild decay, the rank, murky river which continued to feed the pestilence.

He passed rows of shuttered shops and empty homes; passed women in tears and bewildered children. He detested the stench; it made him breathe in short gasps whenever he had no scented cloth in hand.

As the herbs he pulled from fields gave him breath along the river road, so now he would return to his fragrant rose potion. Uncertain of the cause of failure in Agen, he modified the formula and with the aid of those city fathers not stricken by the plague he ordered four thousand roses to be plucked before sunrise; they were pulverized and mixed with one ounce of sawdust from the green cypress. To this he added six ounces of iris of Florence, three ounces of cloves, three drams of odorated calamus. The mixture was placed in the sun to dry, then shaped into lozenges the size of olive pits. Patients were instructed to keep a lozenge in the mouth both day and night.

Perhaps the rose formula was truly a miraculous cure, as many claimed. But Michel had known the illusion of performing miracles before, and so he accepted gratitude with modesty and considered that perhaps the plague had indeed run its course at the time of his arrival. Whatever the cause, he was gratified to see the streets begin to fill with people, and the shops gradually opening at last for business. Once again the streets were tamped clean of weeds by returning commerce.

Michel dictated his prescription to the resident doctors, and continued on to Marseilles. By the time of his arrival, few remained in need of his service. The maritime city was blessed with cleansing winds from the sea, and in this place Michel made a temporary home to gather his thoughts and begin a plan conceived on his journey from Sicily. It was to be an almanac, an application of his astral studies to the larger world and its cycles of events. A modest project, and one of limited originality, for other such editions were already available; and yet Michel believed that he could infuse an uncommon quality into an established form. It would not tax his strength, and would allow for expansion. If his spirit was capable of greater vision, it would come in time.

III

CONCERNING MATTERS OF COURT, AND WAITING FOR DESTINY

IN the years when Michel sought wisdom, I busied myself with less noble tasks. I sought nothing, and waited for good luck to come my way.

In 1536, true to my uncle's speculation, Henri, Duc d'Orleans, became the heir to the throne when his elder brother, François, died under mysterious circumstances. Some said the cause was simply a huge consumption of ice water following a heated tennis match. Others claimed it was caused by poison placed in the Dauphin's clay drinking jar. A man by the name of Monteculi was accused, in any case, and summarily executed after making a confession wrested from him under most uncomfortable conditions.

By the time of his ascendancy to Dauphin during his eighteenth year, Henri had been married three years, and consistent with early habits, he spent as little time with his wife as possible. He preferred to hunt or play tennis by day; by night, once he had reported to Catherine on the outcome of his day's sport, he would lapse into silence, eat supper with indifference and retire to his chamber alone. Occasionally he made nocturnal visits to his wife, but they were so infrequent that the King blamed Henri for Catherine's lack of fecundity. Toward intimacy he showed only distaste—until the Lady Diane once again entered his life, the lady who appeared like a vision of his mother when first we landed after the long internment in Spain.

When I first became aware of his friendship with the Lady Diane, I remembered how she had held the eleven-year-old boy in her arms on the banks of the Bidassoa. She was thirty-one then, and married to Louis de Brezé, governor of Normandie; six years later she was widowed and soon became a frequent visitor to the court at Saint-Germain-en-Laye.

Unlike François's *mignons,* the young and frivolous girls with whom he surrounded himself, Diane was intelligent and mature; a woman not valued for the moment, but for her classical grace. She had made an art of preserving feminine charm in a world of changing, youthful faces. Even at thirty-seven she was a handsome woman, and though her hair was prematurely silver, even this she turned to advantage by wearing costumes of black and white. It was said that she kept her skin radiant and fair by bathing only in cool water, and it was said that beneath the layers of fashionable silks her body remained as taut and slim as the ever-youthful Huntress, her namesake. With Diane in her role as Diana, eternal nymph, eternal mother, the Dauphin found a solace unattainable with his shy, coarse-featured bride.

Her gravity and wise counsel attracted Henri, as did her idealism, her professed fidelity to the Roman Church and her widow's fidelity to the memory of her husband. She was a symbol of faith and stability to Henri, who thought his father incapable of loyalty or conviction since his sympathy for Roman or Protestant ways vacillated with each new opportunity to requisition gold from German princes, Parliament or Pope.

The ardor of the 1544 treaty of Soissons soon dimmed. The King wore his golden collar (presented to him by the King of Spain) for an occasional state dinner, but as time passed it became increasingly difficult for him to honor his pledges. There were incidents; Charles transgressed. François stayed by the treaty, though Henri regarded his father's resolve as temporary.

"He will break the treaty. My father cannot keep a promise; the very looseness of his facile tongue is proof of a heart that shall never hold true to course," Henri said flatly one day as I was accompanying him to Diane's estate at Anet, a few hours by coach from Paris. "He writhes in a bondage of vows. Whenever Charles infringes on French soil, as if to convince himself, he says to me: 'When you do a generous thing, my son, you must do it completely and boldly,' but he only bolsters himself until the next Spanish sortie will allow him to break his oath."

Broken promises. Shattered vows. Henri would prefer to live in the age of knights and Crusades, a time (he believed) when vows could only be broken by death. The Lady Diane was his mistress in the manner of old: a goddess not to be sullied by worldly love. Did she not wear her widow's garb, foreswearing colorful costume? Had she not erected a monument to her husband in Rouen and pledged upon its unveiling that she would honor him by remaining always in mourning?

Ironically, when Diane broke her vow by becoming Henri's lover, Henri was only too ready to accept his lady's rather technical explanation: "I promised only to remain in mourning, and so I shall, for I shall always wear black."

Overshadowed by his father, at pains to avoid his wife, Henri established a routine which carried him through the next several years while he waited for the day when the death of his father would bring him into power. The year after the treaty of Soissons, Henri became the only possible male heir to the French crown when his younger brother, Charles, died during an outbreak of pestilence.

We who attended the Dauphin were in a constant state of packing his garments for journeys to Anet during those years. Away from his father's court, Henri became transformed. At Diane's chateau I saw him as an attentive lover and a disciple of the arts. Her estate was a gathering place for poets and philosophers; I yearned to be accepted as a poet and musician among them, though my first duty always remained attending to Henri's needs.

In Diane's eyes the presence of poet and philosopher was as essential as fine food and statuary, so these things became important to Henri, although much refinement of phrase and subtlety of theory was lost on him. His favorite book was the romance of Amadis of Gaul; his notion of poetry was simple and narrowly framed; therefore I was surprised when one day as our carriage passed through Rouen upon our return from Anet to Paris, he said: "Teach me to write poetry."

"You have studied the Latin poets," I began, recalling the classical education upon which his father had insisted, and in which I had drilled him as a boy.

"All I can manage is a weak copy of Cicero or Ovid."

"Then write from your heart," I said. "At first it will read awkwardly, but as you delve within for words to portray your sentiments, soon the words will spring to mind with slight bidding and the poem will write itself."

"On the other hand, perhaps I should perfect my Latin," he muttered. "Lady Diane seems to hold scholars in high esteem."

"But French is your tongue," I protested, returning to my usual stance on this subject. "There are scholars enough. If I may say so, the scholarly role does not suit you as a man who loves the freedom of a hunt, the freshness of nature."

"In one language or another I must write of my love for her when I am away. I pace like a caged lion," he said, turning in the seat for one last glimpse of Normandie countryside before our carriage turned onto the Paris road. We sat in silence a while, with no sound but the droning of cicadas to accompany our twilight ride.

"Tomorrow I will not see her. Perhaps I will withdraw from our troubled times and consider a greater age. Amadis may bring me to my own muse."

I thought of the neglected Catherine who would spend another night alone if Henri carried out his program of solitary reading. As if in anticipation of my objection he said, "Diane advises me to spend more time with my wife, for as she reminds me, one day Catherine will be Queen and mother of my heirs."

Henri's sadness diminished with each sojourn to Anet. While François held court in the Louvre, in Fontainebleau, in the chateaux of the Loire amidst silken crowds of girls and clusters of courtiers, Henri held court in Normandie surrounded by myths of another age.

The sculptures adorning Lady Diane's garden were cast in the image of Diana and the Stag. Among chestnut and maple trees the slender goddess gazed down; she graced the visitor with her ever chaste and beguiling smile. From paintings on the walls, frescoes on the ceiling, on the sensuously curved vases, the inlaid faces of clocks and the vast expanse of tapestries, one was almost overwhelmed with studies of the goddess in her many guises. Sometimes she was portrayed with a slim, boyish body while other times she was shown as a tender motherly figure with ample breasts who cared for the gentle forest creatures.

Within the grounds and halls of Anet, one could never forget Diana. Her legend filled Henri's eyes when they shared intimate moments within her bedchamber. While the real Diane lay beneath silken coverlets, Henri saw beyond her to the posters of the great bed where four winsome goddesses gazed ardently toward him. Each day bore a feast of poetry and entertainment, delicacies prepared expressly to Henri's—not François's—taste. It was a kingdom with no other King or Queen, a place where schedules of court were dismissed, except that supreme program determined by Henri's whim. While life at Anet revolved around him, Diane quietly groomed him to her specifications both as her lover and as eventual King.

As the old order neared an end the King ringed himself more closely with beauty, as though the vitality of youth could somehow delay his passing. He lay in his grand bed, stricken face ghastly against a constantly changing mound of soft white pillows.

When sunset approached on what proved his last

day, I was called to his room where I sat on the far side of the chamber and played softly upon my lute while the changing parade glided by in elegant gowns, stopping at his bedside for a last farewell.

Midevening, a page was sent for Henri. I overheard the King tell his physicians that he was profoundly weak; it was essential to speak to his son at once.

Henri entered the room and made a slight bow, one properly respectful yet distant. The tragedy of the moment did not serve to counterbalance years of resentment, bitter memories of Spain, the favoritism shown his elder brother, a lifetime of misunderstandings.

"Move close to me and listen well," François said faintly; Henri stood rigidly by the bedside.

"In earlier days when my mind was clear, I spoke to you of the craft of kingship. You may disregard those words from defiance, or you may have forgotten them. But if you remember only two things when I am gone...first, retain my able counselors and seek their seasoned advice. Think of them not as an extension of me, but as your inheritance. Value them thus as men who possess great stores of wisdom and the keenest of judgment. You would be discarding a fortune, if you discharge these good men."

Henri stood uneasily by his father's bed and gave no reply.

"Second," the King spoke so softly I had to strain to hear across the room. "Learn from my mistakes," he said. "If you disregard my words, I promise you misfortune. My life has been determined by women, by my mother, sister, and others less enduring but no less formidable. Do not allow *this* woman to control your life."

"This woman you speak of has the mind of a man," Henri said curtly. "She offers better counsel than the squabbling old men you bequeath to me as royal advisers; moreover, her loyalty to me is absolute. Her wish is only that I might be fulfilled; for herself she seeks no crown."

The King raised himself with great difficulty, weighted as he was by layers of embroidered quilts.

"She may seek no crown, but her avarice is commonly known."

"I refuse to listen to your abuse," Henri said, palm held toward the King like a shield against unwelcome words. "Soon it shall be my exclusive right to listen to whomever I choose and similarly bestow my favors. Does it matter if I shower one lady with gifts rather than a hundred, as you did? Even if I am absurdly generous with her, it will cost the treasury less than if I had your painted hordes to pamper and please."

François collapsed on his pillows and closed his eyes. I tensed with concern but noticed his breathing was even, neither had it ceased nor was it especially labored; I understood that he was gathering strength for resolution.

I looked upon the dying father and the defiant son, and though I am not a religious man, yet I prayed for the grace of reconciliation in these last minutes of a shared life. Into the angry silence I urged the softest possible music from my instrument.

At last the King sighed, breaking the silence.

"I see there dawns a new regime."

My music filled the empty space until Henri whispered, "The new regime may be less grand than yours, but I can only be who I am. I promise to consider your advice, yet finally I will act as my conscience bids."

"...finally, I cannot ask for more."

Pleasing Henri lay worlds beyond the many talents of Catherine. Truly she had perfect manners and a keen mind; with meticulous grooming and lavish gowns, she even succeeded in disguising her unattractive figure; but she was continually somber, and perhaps this was the single key to her failure as Henri's wife.

It was less her plainness that repulsed him than the quality he saw in her: an image of himself, the motherless and almost fatherless child. In Marseilles when he had first looked into the face of the orphaned girl, pawn of her papal uncle, he found no light or hope. They had both known imprisonment and resignation as children; Henri turned inward and found solace in a brooding piety and, later, he found consolation in the arms of his mistress Diane. As she matured, Catherine searched the words of sorcerers and seers for some sign of future happiness: "Will I bear children?" she asked the astrologers. "Will I ever be Queen?"

Catherine's first ten years of marriage had been barren, and for this the citizens of Paris cursed the Florentine for bringing bad blood to the royal family. They almost convinced Catherine that she was tainted until, discouraged, she had sought an audience with her father-in-law, the King. There she offered to commit herself to a convent so that Henri might remarry and provide France with an heir. But when she made this offer the King refused her request and a curse seemed to lift, for she believed he had faith in her after all. Within a year she bore Henri a daughter. In following years there were two more daughters, then her first son. In fulfilling her role as mother, she earned the right to be Queen of all France, despite the woman who held her husband's love.

Gossip and petty stories about Catherine were plentiful in the compound of Anet, where I spent a great deal of time in attendance to the Dauphin. Word had it that Lady Diane had a platoon of spies who observed Catherine's daily actions. Her primary purpose in this was to control the education of the royal children. Perhaps one might call this a rather grandmotherly interest, for she was of just that age in relation to the royal offspring; perhaps her interest was due to Diane's self-appointed godmothership, for it was at her insistence that Henri had entered his wife's bedchamber. In any case, it became the special concern of Diane de Poitiers to select and manipulate the attendants who provided the royal children's education.

Surely the Queen was aware of this; it was rumored that she watched her husband's clandestine lovemaking, when Diane visited the palace, through a peephole in the ceiling of the lovers' suite. And in the face of their public dalliance, though her stoicism was remarkable, this strong façade must have masked a sad, sick heart. Her rival was formidable. Diane offered Henri a temple in which he could worship and find peace, and her favors were administered with the detail of an accomplished priestess. She proffered answers when Henri came to her needing advice; she offered herself when he came needing love. But she demanded much of him, and like the goddess of antiquity that was her namesake, she required devotion.

On the day of Henri's coronation, he impulsively ordered that Diane was to be crowned at his side. His father's advisers fought against such an outrage of custom and law, but he claimed he was otherwise unable to perform the anointing ceremony. At the last, when their legal wills prevailed, he made one final effort.

As I helped him prepare for the coronation, he turned to me in distress and said, "I must send her a message, that I shall always be her subject and her servant, never her ruler."

"Your Highness, hold still," I interjected, slipping an ermine mantle across his shoulders.

"Give me paper and ink," he said, pushing me aside. "I must send her this, or I cannot accept the crown."

Immediately I brought paper and writing material, then watched as his hand flew across the parchment, his lips moving in a whisper until the sheet was filled, his confession spent.

"The page will help me dress," he said. "I need you for the more important duty of finding the Lady Diane."

Time was precious. I took the folded and sealed letter, ran swiftly through the door.

"I rely on you!" he called as I ran from his chamber.

It was a difficult task. The Lady Diane was somewhere in the mob that filled the Cathedral of Rheims, where the royal party had journeyed for the coronation. Beyond the throng of commoners outside, it seemed that all the nobility of France and half that of Europe were within the walls. If I searched for her by myself, I knew there would be only a slim chance of finding her. I needed a whole force of helpers to conduct the search for me, while I remained in one place awaiting their reports.

With the folded letter and its royal seal as my authority, I recruited two score of young boys to go into the crowd, charged with the task of finding a beautiful lady with light hair, dressed in black and white.

At that moment I offered a prayer of gratitude for Lady Diane's hypocritical mourning costume. It was surely by her dress and her beauty that one of the boys discovered Diane de Poitiers and led me to her, back through the crowd.

"His Majesty sends this letter and begs you to read it at once," I said, slipping it into her gloved hand. I averted my glance as she gently pulled apart the seal and read it, then she refolded the letter and placed it in the folds of her cape.

"Go to him at once," she smiled. "Tell him all is well. Nothing shall change between us."

Three days later I accompanied the King to Anet. As we rode through the countryside, he tapped his fingers restlessly on the carriage seat.

I played music while they dined on dainty quail at a small candlelit marble table in Diane's private chamber. Only I and one of Diane's trusted maidservants remained to freshen their wineglasses and to tend the fire.

"Nothing will change," said Henri, reaffirming his message as he clasped Diane's hand.

"I only agreed to appease you yesterday," she smiled, "for you shall change and you must; you must swell in power until you fill France with your spirit. You will be a triumphant ruler, my dear. The people shall celebrate your reign for decades to come."

"Why must I change to accomplish this? Is it not enough that I am crowned and anointed?"

"No... you lack, forgive me, magnificence. Show them grandeur and the people will lay down their lives. But show them you are weak and inconsequential, and the country will crumble around you."

"What exactly do you propose, to create the illusion of a magnificent reign?"

Her eyes danced with designs. "I propose that you stage a series of triumphal entries—a grand tour of your kingdom. Enter each city like a victorious Roman emperor and those who witness such a spectacle will long remember you and speak of you to their children. In this manner you shall capture the imagination and the will of the people; they shall lose their hearts to you, as have I."

"I prefer to celebrate in Paris, with jousts and tourneys. I am willing to tilt against the best men, and in this way show my prowess. My love, I am not a pagan emperor. I shall be a knight, a Crusader."

"But tourneys are of the past, my dear. First, you are more than a knight, you are the liege. Second, there is no Crusade to be won at present—but there *are* lands to be regained. Lands lost by your father. You need not be pagan to control an empire." Her voice softened. "And to love the beauty of the antique is not pagan. Does not the art of antiquity and its poetry serve the imagination of today?"

"How can I deny this, my goddess?"

"You may have the power of antique festivals and increase the love of your people, and you may have piety too. With both on your side, your rule shall be double the magnitude of your father's."

* * *

December 17, 1547

My Dear Alain,

I trust this letter finds you in good health and that you continue to benefit from the courtly life. For my part, I have married again, to a widow of unswerving virtue and considerable means. Her name is Anne Poinsard Gemelle. We have established residence in her house on the Place de la Poissonerie in Salon.

I received Michel's letter in early spring of 1548; he wrote that he was now living in greater comfort than he had ever imagined, with the effect that he no longer was obligated to earn a livelihood. At last he could reduce his practice to a few patients and instead of "tending boils" was able to devote himself to other pursuits. Two years later he wrote again, detailing his accomplishments:

among them, the completion of an almanac: the conventional kind, with advice as to the phases of the moon when seed should be sown and crops gathered, also auspicious times for other ventures.

He explained that the almanac had been well-received in Provence, though he admitted to a certain embarrassment at its popular success since he regarded the work as a modest effort. He was more enthusiastic about another project—an expanded almanac—and said he had been experimenting with new modes of expression. The direct prose form of the almanac, he complained, could only allow him to convey limited and pedestrian information, information Michel could readily calculate with the use of his astrological tables and charts. He remarked that the ease of accomplishment and a certain degree of boredom had provoked him to polish up his languages. It sounded as though the result was a patchwork prose style with the substitution of Latin and Greek words for French; he insisted this technique would distinguish his prognostications from those of other almanacs.

Long ago my grandfather taught me to prefer Plato's truth to Aristotle's neat categories. Common knowledge is but shadows on the mind's wall; the language of symbols and oblique expression are better suited to higher pursuits. But need I point this out to a poet?

At the time his explanation was confusing, but I could appreciate the disciplines he was imposing upon himself. He began a translation of Horapollo's treatise on Egyptian hieroglyphics. When this was completed, he then concentrated on Latin by translating a detailed description of an Italian wedding feast and a section of Galen.

As I read his letter, I detected a scattering of interests, and this impression was confirmed a few lines later when he wrote:

If it can be called a curse in the midst of contentment, then I am cursed by only one thing: distraction.

Free at last to edit the notes he had collected on compounds and medications, Michel abandoned the Galen translation midway through to edit his pharmacological notes. Along his journeys, many unusual recipes found their way into his notebooks, among them restoratives, cosmetics and confitures, including the ingredients for the quince jelly Michel enjoyed on his last night in Toulouse.

Intent upon proving the worth of such recipes, he began to oversee the making of confitures and sweets in his wife's kitchen and the preparation of restoratives whose formulas he had procured over the past years. So effective were the latter that his wife, delighted with the cosmetic effects, offered samples to her many friends. To put an end to a phase he considered to have been taken up by "wasteful dilettantism," Michel handed his edited collection of prescriptions, recipes and restoratives to a printer, who suggested that for commercial purposes the title should be *Treatise on Cosmetics*. The manuscript was so unwieldy that the printer recommended publishing a slim edition first which, if it earned back the cost of production, would indicate that a second and possibly third volume should follow to utilize the already prepared notes.

Shortly after I received Michel's account of his new life and undertakings, I learned that the King had taken Lady Diane's advice, and plans for a grand tour of France were already under way. Theatrics have never been my forte, but during the next months of preparation I learned about the staging of such a series of events. The cost of it was astonishing, and what was spent on the hundreds of yards of silks, velvet, lace, feathers, and other novelties could have kept the entire populace of Paris well-clothed for a year. Instead, these costumes were to be worn by the royal family and the hundred attendants who would comprise a kind of traveling show; the costumes would transform our King and his itinerant court into a tableau of classical personages with their appropriately garbed retainers.

Finally, all the details were ready. Carriages and conveyances were decorated and packed with basic provisions (fresh meats, produce, cheese and wine would be secured along the way). I took my place in the third carriage behind the King's own, and considered the problem of keeping my white gladiator's tunic clean for the duration of the three-month journey, but this was a problem forgotten in the first triumphal entry when dust from carriage wheels and horses' hooves covered commoner and King alike; we simply shook them out and wore them again in the next town on our route.

By far the most impressive of the triumphal entries was that staged in Lyons. Cheering townspeople lined the streets as the King's cavalcade paraded by. At the fore, the monarch rode tall and grand in a suit which simulated Roman armor, and at his side reclined the elegantly gowned Lady Diane.

The line of carts decked with blossoms and banners slowly rolled past, bearing noblemen and court officials dressed in splendid ceremonial attire. Each cart was more dust-laden than the one before, and at the end of the train (scheduled to pass through Lyons's triumphal arch so late in the afternoon that it was nearly dusk) rode the Queen, her homely face barely visible in the fading light.

Since the King's party would remain in Lyons for a week, I was granted three days to visit my family in Saint-Rémy. I rode out on the first night after the triumphal entry and by daybreak I was once again in my childhood home.

My parents were old now, and my father's hair had turned white; he walked with the aid of a mahogany cane. My mother was well and much as I'd remembered, even though the years had etched in permanence the kindly lines around her eyes. My taunting sister was now the mother of two children and it was odd to hear two young strangers calling me "Uncle Alain!" My sister chided me gently for the number and brevity of the letters I had sent over the years.

The reunion, though brief, was joyous, and when I departed on the second day I knew that I desired to spend my later years not in a cold stone dwelling in

Paris, but in the sweet-scented, windswept land of Provence.

From Saint-Rémy it was not a hard ride to Michel's home in Salon. I had but one more day of leave from my duties and decided that if I rode my horse all night on the return to Lyons, I could take a day to visit him.

I arrived in Salon as the moon was rising. To a lone man hurrying down the street I called out, "Where is the home of Michel de Nostredame?"

"Oh, the husband of the Widow Gemelle," he replied after a moment, then pointed. "Her home is the large one, just up the way."

Indeed it was a handsome home; Michel had married well.

"Alain!" he cried, surprised at seeing me, for I had had no time to send a message ahead. Inside the foyer he stood back as if to see me more clearly, then shook his head in disbelief. "After all these years—you've hardly changed."

I had, of course, and my once-boyish features had not been dignified by the accumulation of years. For Michel it was just the opposite. At forty-five years of age he was a man of great dignity; his girth added stature and authority where he had once been overly lean. At his temples and along the perimeter of his beard were handsome areas of gray that reminded me of an artist's rendering of the wise men of old. Had Michel lived at court like me, he would have extinguished this dignifying characteristic with dye, and would have been the poorer for its loss.

"Come, I will introduce you to my wife. She already knows all about you and calls you 'my student friend.' She will ask a thousand questions about Paris."

We entered a larger room, richly furnished and hung with tapestries. In a large upholstered chair sat Madame Nostredame, swollen with child.

"Anne, we have a visitor. May I present Alain Saint-Germain."

"At last!" she said, offering me her hand. It was warm and firm; I could not but help contrasting it to Madeleine's.

We exchanged pleasantries over glasses of Provençal wine and after a while she excused herself, saying, "I must get my rest now. We had several guests for dinner tonight and though they did not linger, I am tired from the effort."

I could see into yet another room where servants appeared to be polishing silver serving pieces. After she was gone Michel said, "The social sphere of the new Madame Nostredame encompasses bishop and barrister, jeweler and printer, and minor nobility as well. Almost every night our dining table is set for a dozen guests; as host, I find I am urged by these provincial visitors to recount tales of my 'travels and triumphs.' To my surprise, they praise me as a first-rate teller of tales."

"It is easy for a man of intelligence to capture any audience with a mixture of imagery and measured phrase. This is my calling, but not yours. What of your studies?"

"Three years have vanished with nothing to show for it but an almanac which any simpleton could compile, and a treatise on cosmetics. Our home is constantly bustling with guests and I seem unable to concentrate."

"Surely in this large house you could use a quiet room for your library," I remarked.

"I have been reluctant to suggest it. Anne has long been mistress of her home, and she takes great pride in its appointment."

It was comforting to be in his presence again and as we spoke the intervening years compressed into an evening's conversation. He told me at length of his vagabond years, of the man at the thermal baths who had led him to Thières in Lorraine; of the traveler whose vulgar words offered a clue to his teacher Giolo, the master of birds; of how he was sent from Venice to the recluse in Sicily who taught him to read the message of smoke.

And though Michel had warned me of his wife's curiosity, he himself asked many questions about the court and of my service to Uncle Léon, in particular of my impressions of Louis de Condé, who was leader of the Protestant party, and of François, Duc de Guise.

"Why do such matters interest you?" I asked.

"Anne's circle includes a cardinal of the region. Often we sup and he delights in telling of matters relayed by his own network of informers. I frequently cast horoscopes for him."

"The upper echelons of the clergy are second to none for plotting," I observed.

"Even though I have regarded the cardinal as an annoying dinner guest, I admit that in casting the star charts of such highly placed persons I find that more speculations on the future of France are finding their way into my notebooks."

On that note he rose and paced the floor, as if his rhythmic strides could carry him to a conclusion. I continued to talk a while, then noticed he was not listening. Eventually I began to doze.

"Forgive me, my friend," Michel said when presumably I began to snore. "You are tired and I have become lost in my own preoccupations. Let me call the servant to prepare your bed."

A while later as I lay on the cot, I wondered whether I had wrongly inspired Michel as I heard him address Anne:

"I must give up these diversions and resume my work. I need privacy and a quiet place to work, away from the incessant traffic of servants cleaning up after the last entertainment and immediately preparing for the next."

"But you have promised your rosewater and creams to our friends," I heard Anne say, a note of bewilderment in her voice. "Are you not happy?"

"I seek only peace, and to gain it I must break a few promises. I will no longer be a hireling to justify a luxurious life."

I heard nothing more; apparently Michel had rather harshly made his point.

Nothing further was said of this matter as we ate our breakfast of porridge and cream. Anne appeared subdued, while Michel treated her with special tenderness and I surmised that he regretted stating his case too plainly. After the meal, Anne excused herself to attend to other household details and an unexpected visitor appeared at the door.

The young man introduced himself as Adam de Craponne.

"I come to you, Doctor Nostradamus, as the only man in Salon capable of understanding my vision."

"What is this 'vision'?" asked Michel, trying to disguise his amusement, for the young man appeared to be a simple rustic lad with a whimsical shock of red hair that stuck up in a wayward tuft.

"The land of Salon is dry, but on either side of the plain, the Rhône and Soare rivers flow like blue borders around us and waste their nourishment in the sea. Doctor Nostradamus, I believe that if we divert water from these rivers, we shall create a pattern of waterways across the plain and the arid land around Salon will become a verdant garden."

"What profit do you seek for your effort?" asked Michel.

"I expect no profit, except to irrigate my father's land and that of his townspeople. You have applied unconventional methods in your medical practice, I have heard; I therefore come to you for help."

Without agreeing, Michel said he would consider underwriting the venture. Adam smiled appreciatively, showing a row of uneven teeth, and pulled a cap back on top of his unruly hair.

"I know you must leave soon, but let us ride out to the plain, for I would like your opinion on this matter," Michel said to me after Adam had departed.

We rode beyond the half-timbered buildings of the town, into a countryside of small fields surrounded by a vast expanse of weed and coarse brush struggling to grow in sun-hardened earth.

"This improbable project interests me," Michel said. "I have often dreamed of a waterway. Sometimes I see it from above, like the warp and woof of some exquisite fabric; other times in my dream it appears as dried brown scars on the earth, then the marks turn to inked lines on parchment, rippling lines of words extending in all directions."

I saw the distant look in his eyes and recalled last night's discussion; yet here was another distraction, another project tempting him away from concentration.

"It seems to me that you can well afford to give the young man both money and encouragement if you think there is merit to his plan," I suggested. "But Michel, this is *his* vision. I beseech you to return to the pursuit of your own."

During the slow journey back to Paris, which was delayed by Henri's fancy to spend a month at the chateau of Blois, I often brooded upon the fate which had granted Michel two families, even though one had been lost to him, while I remained alone. When Michel wrote me of the birth of his son, it occurred to me that I might also have a son or daughter, though I had given the matter little thought for several years.

The incident which made my parenthood possible was a second assignation with the Lady Yvette, she whom I had first romanced in a coach house when I was barely more than a boy. Unexpectedly, a long while later, the lady had approached me with more serious intent, for her marriage to a respectable but much older gentleman had not been fruitful, and on her husband she lay the blame.

Flattered to be chosen as surrogate, I agreed to meet her at the inn of Saint-Michel. When it was over, she thanked me and returned to her husband, and I gave little mind to the consequences. But now that Michel had sired a child in his forty-fifth year, my own loneliness or vanity or a combination thereof was stirred. After a few discreet inquiries I found that indeed the Lady Yvette had a fair-haired son. As small consolation to myself, and as a boast to Michel, I wrote him of the child, though once I had placed the letter with a traveler bound for Provence, I regretted this candor and knew his next letter would be far from congratulatory. To my surprise, many months later he wrote:

My Dear Alain,

I understand the pride of siring a son, and I do not judge you ill for the circumstances of his conception; indeed, you have discreetly provided an heir for another man who would otherwise have none.

My own son, who is unmistakably of my own blood and who bears his father's gray eyes, was nonetheless baptized with another man's given name and one which may seem unlikely to you. I have named him César, for though his namesake was weak when persuaded that his reputation was under threat, overall he was a man of great learning. I wish this for my son.

Michel continued to describe the events which had transpired since our last meeting.

The walls dividing several chambers were torn aside to create one large room in the house. This room has become a library, study and sleeping room combined, according to my specifications. Though Anne objects, there are many nights when a bare cot affords greater repose than would my wife's soft bed.

From the second story he could see across the rooftops of Salon, gaze unobstructed into the night sky where fiery constellations slowly progressed past his study window. He worked by a portable coal fire, his legs wrapped in a blanket through long chilled nights until the morning star reminded him to close his books and claim needed rest. Surrounding Michel were cherished manuscripts guarded with care since his student days in Avignon, and others which dated from the years when he studied at Jean de Saint-Rémy's side.

He lined the walls with these treasures whose pages were much-turned and worn. To these he added more rare books, some ferreted from bookstalls in Lyons, some from teachers with whom he had made contact through cautiously phrased letters. His library grew; night after night he read unaware of time until collapsing for a few hours of restless sleep.

* * *

Michel wrote with elation soon thereafter, describing the night when decades of study and discouragement were replaced by a moment of clarity:

One night, from a cupboard behind my cot I removed a porphyry bowl. Years ago I had filled it with wood to evoke the message of smoke. But on this night I poured in pure water and set it upon a tripod by the study window. On the liquid surface, unmarred by breeze, I saw reflections of the room around me. Such images were in reverse: the inverted window frame, the intersecting lines of a pane, an earthy brown blur from the leather books on a nearby shelf.

I looked upon the surface, my eyesight diffused by the twisted images until I no longer saw an inverted room but only a net of watery shapes. Thus the great work came forth, and from images on water the spirit of its message crystallized into the first quatrain:

> Seated at night in my private chamber
> > Alone, bent over the tripod of brass
> A slender flame arises from solitude
> > Urging forth that which shall not
> > > be in vain professed.

> Poised in the center of the tripod
> > With scepter I anoint my foot and hand
> In fear I commence to tremble
> > Heavenly Splendor; the divine wisdom
> > > is at my side

Michel's unusual hours brought accusations from the townspeople of Salon who believed that anyone pondering over books until sunrise could only be a practitioner of black arts. Another rumor spread, a rumor which had followed Michel along his travels: it was said that Michel de Nostredame was secretly practicing Jewish rites.

During daylight hours when he chanced to look from the study window, often Michel saw someone glaring at him from the cobbled street below. Or, if there were two men standing on the street and if one saw Michel appear at his window, an accusing finger would point upward as if to say, "There he is now, working his devilry in daylight!"

He detested the townspeople who whispered behind his back in the marketplace, who stared when he passed them on the road; soon Michel stopped walking within the city walls and became a prisoner within his own home.

Yet, despite his detractors, Michel's notebooks swelled. In a short time he had completed five sections of a work he envisioned as ten groupings in its completed form, with each section containing a hundred verses. Though the five completed sections contained material which, if correctly read, would not find favor with the King, nonetheless Michel believed the work should be offered to anyone of a disposition to look upon the future and he trusted to the indirectness of the language to protect him.

With the success of the almanacs, and the surprising (to Michel) popularity of his treatise on recipes and restoratives, an arrangement was easily made with an excellent printer in Lyons, Macé Bonhomme. After a disagreement in which the printer's agent insisted that only four of the five sections would fit into the allotted signatures, the manuscript was set in type in the abbreviated form to which Michel reluctantly agreed, and a first edition of *The Prophecies of Michel de Nostredame* was to appear in the booksellers stall in the winter of 1555.

Late one morning Anne entered Michel's study with a bowl of water and a towel, only to find him fast asleep, for he had exhausted himself by reading a treatise on Ptolemaic astronomy throughout the night.

"Bonhomme's agent has arrived," she said, shaking him gently. "He brings good news."

Michel rose and splashed the cool water onto his face, rubbing away the heaviness of sleep with a rough towel, then he reached for his soiled robe.

"Wear this clean robe," she said, handing him a freshly brushed garment. The room was musty, the chamberpot had not been emptied for two days, as Michel had requested no interruptions.

"You look poorly," Anne said, opening a window to air the room. "I am concerned for your health."

Cool air from the window revived him; indeed it seemed days since he had last descended the stairs.

"Doctor Nostradamus!" the printer's agent called cheerfully when Michel entered the room. *"The Prophecies* are a remarkable success. We have sold out all copies of our first printing, so I took the liberty of producing more. Please give me your answer regarding the second edition so that I may announce it."

Michel sat in silence until Anne asked if he was feeling unwell.

"Not unwell, only concerned," he replied, for he had been forewarned in a dream that great difficulties would attend his work and he looked upon public acceptance with mistrust.

"Yes, you may announce a second volume," Michel said at last. "Even now my notebooks contain material for the next edition, and for yet another. I need only edit my notes."

"Excellent," said the agent, "now let us speak of revenue."

"I shall represent my Michel in this matter, that he may be free to concentrate upon his work," said Anne. The agent sighed, knowing she would draw a hard bargain. As Michel returned to his study he heard the printer mention a figure, to which Anne replied, "Come now, surely every printer between Salon and Paris would seize an opportunity to publish my husband's work."

That afternoon when Michel had bathed and had eaten his first full meal in two days, his mood was too expansive to be contained within the dark house. He closed the door of his chamber, descended the stairs and walked alone into the streets of Salon. True, he heard the usual whisperings from the townspeople, but that day they angered him no more than the droning cicadas in the surrounding fields.

The name of Nostradamus was oft mentioned in Paris during the early part of 1556, for in March a comet appeared and gave immediate credence to the quatrain which prophesied:

> While the star with the bright tail is seen
> Three great princes will verge on war
> Peace will be dealt a blow from the heavens
> Po and Tiber's floods shall leave a serpent
> on the shore.

During the three months that the comet lit the skies, truce between France and Spain was broken, the Tiber and Arno overflowed and on the banks of the Tiber—so the reports confirmed—a huge snakelike fish was found.

"While the star with the bright tail is seen" became an idiom for verity, and the book itself was the darling of the moment; not only were courtiers and nobility its readers, but merchants and craftsmen also showed appetite for the curious poems that foretold of intrigue, wars, catastrophies and the fate of many states besides France. *The Prophecies* was quoted, analyzed, interpreted in gatherings among all members of society. Yet there were some who refused to bow to fashion, and looked upon the work as an inspiration of Satan.

Within two years of the first edition, the complete volume appeared, composed of the first seven sections plus a final three; *The Prophecies* now consisted of ten sections of one hundred quatrains, called by chapter headings as "centuries."

For a long while I told no one of my friendship with Michel, so controversial was his book; or rather I told no one except my uncle, for he could be trusted not to reveal our bond.

Over the years, Léon had become a rather placid old man. Gone was his once passionate interest in the maneuverings of the court, as though under Henri's reign he was content to relax his vigil. Though he had long since withdrawn from society and commerce, Léon still loved to parry a point; it was my duty as his nephew and closest residing kin to provoke an occasional discussion.

One night we sat together in his library after a meal of grouse stuffed with oysters, and the groom who had once annoyed me (and who had matured into a faithful manservant) had just replenished my cup.

When conversation flagged, I opened *The Prophecies* and turned to a passage I had pondered that afternoon and found most fascinating:

> The unhappy nuptial shall be celebrated
>> With great joy, but with sadness at last
> The mother shall despise the daughter, Mary
>> The Apollo dies; our pity is vast.

"I find this verse especially provocative," I said, "for Mary, the Scots Queen who resides at court, is not favored by Queen Catherine, mother of Mary's betrothed. He, the Dauphin, may grow into a handsome 'Apollo,' however, and if this quatrain foreshadows their unhappy marriage, then surely his death is indicated."

Léon asked to see the passage. "Since Nostradamus likes to bewilder the reader with nouns which are verbs and vice versa, I wonder if there is another meaning. Consider that 'mary' could also mean 'married man,' and if so your entire reading is incorrect."

I granted his point and remarked at the ease of interpretation once I had a key word in mind. It was as though the surrounding verses bent to my understanding.

I selected two more quatrains, but at first he said nothing in response to them, and I thought our discussion had ended for the night. But I was wrong.

"These verses about 'hollow mountains in the New City' and of 'men waging war from the belly of a fish' indeed arouse my interest," he began, and then drew an odd conclusion: "Since these verses have power over the imagination, I wonder if it is possible for an evil man to render convincing meanings, only to suit his malevolent purpose?"

I dismissed my uncle's speculation as an old man's foolish notion and turned to another quatrain, since far future seemed Léon's preference.

> In the year 1999 and seven months
>> From above shall descend a terrifying King
> To restore the great leader d'Angolmois
>> Fore and after, war shall rage without cease.

"I would not brood over this passage," said Léon, "the date is symbolic, given the similarity to the Number of the Beast in Revelation, that is, an inversion of 666."

"Symbolic or no, what kind of terrifying king would descend from the skies? A demi-god? A man with wings? And some say the word 'angolmois' is an anagram for the Mongols. Whenever this occurs, the world can be sure of a period of Oriental terror."

"I understand they are a fastidious people, when it comes to keeping accounts. Perhaps an Oriental reign would be orderly," said Léon with an amused smile. "Speaking of accounts, I am concerned for an overdue payment from a relative of the Prince of Condé. Have you heard any rumors in court concerning the Bourbons?"

I had underestimated his interest in politics, but this was not a case of future speculation and only his worry over a payment from the past.

"No rumors, Uncle, but there happens to be a quatrain in the Third Century of this book which everyone is sure refers to the hunchback Bourbon Prince of Condé." I skimmed the pages and found it; the twenty-fourth verse:

> The hunchback will be chosen by council
>> No more unsightly creature was ever seen
> A deliberately fired shot will enter the eye
>> Of a traitor who has forsworn fealty to his King.

"If this portends the death of 'Bossu' the hunchback as a traitor," I began. Uncle Léon drew his own conclusion.

"Then it does not bode well for repayment of his cousin's debt, does it?"

The discussion with Léon that night was only one of many such conversations in which I found myself en-

gaged. Despite the impressive "comet" quatrain, people
who fancied themselves intellectuals of one kind or another loved to criticize Michel's technique. They usually
fell into one of two groups: those who considered Nostradamus a pretentious impostor or those who regarded
him as an inept poet.

Lady Diane and those who curried her favor adopted
the latter position.

The chateau of the King's mistress near Anet was
awash with various sophists and poets who arrived by
invitation and remained as long as did Diane's pleasure
in their presence. The food was good, rooms not too
crowded, and competition for the honor assured her of a
changing assortment. By 1556 I considered myself a per-
manent member of this troupe, even though much of my
time was necessarily spent in Paris at the official court.

Nightly, Lady Diane would summon the band of sages
and wits who had groomed themselves and were prepared to hold forth on several subjects. When a dozen
men and occasionally a woman or two had gathered in
the great salon, someone would then propose a topic
whereupon we were expected to debate in a dainty fashion, never forgetting that our peers were unimportant;
our real audience consisted of a powerful patroness
and a rather narrow-minded King, so that each man
threaded his way through the pitfalls of language and
logic, trying to avoid connotations which might offend
King Henri.

Rarely did the King or his mistress enter into our
discussions. I am tempted to call the discussions a performance, for the desired effect was one of entertainment and diversion for the King. Perhaps my longevity
as resident among the group at Anet was due to a role
I had assumed naturally: the role of governor over the
changing troupe. As I came to know the lady over many
years, I knew that she favored harmony of opinion,
though within agreement some argumentation was sa-
vored like a pungent bite of pickle during a rich, bland
meal.

I can best illustrate this situation by describing one
evening. After an ordinary hour of music and poetry
followed by a somewhat dry philosophical discussion of

Plotinus (which unfortunately caused the King to doze), I chose a moment when the last and most tedious speaker was sipping a cup of wine and shifted to a newer and livelier topic:

"This Nostradamus, what do you think of the poetic or prophetic content of his work?"

Voices filled the room as the dozen began speaking at once. I had not expected such a passionate response.

"His poetry is abominable," said one, twisting his handsome face into a sneer. "He tortures the quatrain to produce his nefarious 'omens.' I have read only the first few pages. I would not subject myself to more, so obvious did it appear that this charlatan was serving me his bad dreams."

"These are not prophecies," said another man, producing a copy from his doublet (to my surprise). "The event in this verse occurred twenty years ago; I heard the story on my father's knee.

> The Blonde one will war with the Hawk-nose
>   By a duel, he shall be forced to flee
> The exiles will return to their homeland
>   And the strong shall command the seas

"Who else could this mean but Charles of Spain and the hook-nosed Turk who was routed in Tunis twenty years ago? This is no prophecy, but merely a retelling of old tales."

At this point a lady spoke up: "The title itself, *The Prophecies,* means these events have not yet come to pass. It remains for another fair-haired ruler to fulfill the oracle."

"You speak wisely," said a newcomer named Moreau. "Nostradamus speaks truth, though he offers no solace to the mighty who may be cast down."

With this comment the room became silent. Moreau had turned attention to the most provocative of the quatrains, the verses said to predict the death of the King:

> The Young Lion shall overcome the old
>   By one duel in a martial field

His eye shall be rent in a Golden Cage
  Two wounds from one, his cruel death is sealed

"I submit that the first speaker is closer to truth," I said, trying to reinterpret the quatrain harmlessly. "Nostradamus recalls horrible night visions rather than realities, although it is the latter he claims to foretell. He is skilled at contriving puns and in constructing multilayered allusions, and with all this shifting imagery there is more resemblance to dreams than to any event in the world I have known."

Moreau spoke up angrily. "For an alleged poet you are contemptibly far from the mark. Nostradamus speaks the language of prophet and seer, not the language of chronicler or merchant of the fantastical. His images are obscure because his word is revelation and is given for those who have ears to hear." He concluded breathlessly and looked about the room where no one dared meet his eyes.

I sighed; there was little hope of diverting the discussion this evening, for by now it had been ruined by Moreau's frankness. At least I could change the topic to another quatrain, leaving the Old Lion brooding.

"Here...in this passage he predicts the rise of Venice and says she will reach the stature of Rome. Do you think this is possible?" All agreed such an ascent was unlikely. "And here Nostradamus writes of 'an innovation of the age' and from the reckoning of an astronomer's ephemeris I gather from the conjunction of planets mentioned in the subsequent quatrain that this will occur in 1792. But this date is over two hundred years away. Who knows if Nostradamus can see what will happen five years from now or five hundred?"

"I don't intend to be around to find out," said one of the others, with a bored yawn.

Moreau seemed about to open his mouth again, so I tried one more tactic in hope of salvaging the discussion. I tried to isolate Moreau from the rest of us, to reduce him to foolishness and thus save my own skin. The Lady Diane was obviously displeased with me for not monitoring the subject more closely.

"Well then, Moreau," I said, "do you admit to belief in this superstitious prattle? Prattle fit only for men who can neither reason soundly nor create works of art from another place in the soul?"

I caught him off guard with my attack, so certain was Moreau that he had uttered the final word. As he gathered his thoughts, I continued to discredit him:

"Your own poetry strikes me as in no way finding its source in the soul. Thus I may conclude that you do not speak from your soul. Nor are your ill-conceived words guided by reason, for you are as superstitious as a peasant. Thus I conclude you have neither a rational nor an intuitive basis for anything you have said tonight, including your irresponsible statement likening Nostradamus's work to the book of Holy Revelation."

I turned to my royal audience.

"Sir, I plead on this man's behalf that whereas he did speak without benefit of faculties, therefore I recommend that he be forgiven for what amounts to merely an ignorant remark."

The King's grim face softened; we waited for judgment, which came in the form of a deep laugh.

"This man is obviously a fool, as you have made quite plain."

Many said that Nostradamus's prediction concerning the Old Lion had caused the King no small concern. Those of us apprised of this were relieved to make Moreau the scapegoat, though I regretted raising the subject and had done so trusting that no one would take Michel's writings seriously.

"We do not need fools like..."

"Moreau," I said, filling in for the King.

"...thus he is dismissed at once and he shall depart from these grounds before I rise tomorrow."

In the early morning hours Moreau rode away on his horse, a few belongings wrapped in a bundle on his saddle. Until this night he no doubt believed that an invitation to Anet meant a passage to fame and fortune.

Now his banishment saddened me, for though Moreau had incurred his own demise through lack of discernment, it remained that I was the one who contrived his banishment and he was cast out for speaking truth.

As if he could hear my thoughts, or perhaps because his young spirit refused to be dampened by dismissal, Moreau spurred his mount to a lively gallop and soon rode out of sight; it was done.

The sacrifice of Moreau was sufficient weight for my conscience to bear and I vowed that if ever I were called upon to be apologist for Michel, I would defend him to my last word.

In the presence of the King, I took caution to avoid the subject of Michel's work. But another wore the crown and she took great interest in the prophecies.

Long the subject of others' cruelty, Catherine's life must have seemed ill-starred. No wonder that she sought mystical signs of good fortune and consulted seer after seer in hope that one would disclose a consoling future.

When *The Prophecies* was published and word of the work reached her, I happened to be the person most convenient for an errand of such discretion, and so I was dispatched to a bookseller to procure her a copy.

It came as no surprise to me, then, when I heard through the informers of Anet that the Queen had conveyed an invitation to Michel de Nostredame.

If I spoke of Diane's informers as though they were distant, I have given the wrong impression. My life was spent equally in the two courts, and on the road between Paris and Anet. Also I had influential friends and informants of my own on either end of the roadway.

After the many years in court, I found that Uncle Léon's advice was now a part of my fiber, like a language learned when one is young. I had become accomplished in the art of acquiring friends and mutually we provided those details which assured our continued favor.

Did my private life consist only of culling secrets and advancing favors? Regrettably I must answer yes. Long ago I ceased to anguish over poems in a naïve effort to express my "deepest feelings" and when I no longer gave such feelings their due, they ceased to exist. Only on a rare occasion, such as the night I turned out Moreau, did I desire a return to more idealistic times.

I still had many lovers, no longer my own age or older but now all wonderfully youthful, and through them I maintained an illusion of youth. Never did I beg for their company, for I was acknowledged as one of the subtle influences at Henri's side, and thus the young and ambitious ladies (as well as the handsome, ambitious young men) offered me favor for favor. It was an equitable and pleasing arrangement. I squandered no effort on fidelity or vows; I simply plucked those fresh blossoms with little reflection and no regret whenever the opportunity arose.

With my own coterie of friends, it was not difficult to find the man in charge of Michel's accommodations. To repay a favor owed me, the man gladly agreed to provide my friend with especially comfortable quarters in Paris and also the best of inns along his journey, even though the sojourn was to take place in mid-July when roadsides are crowded with fair-weather travelers.

"I have arranged rooms for Doctor Nostradamus at the inn of Saint-Michael," he said. I knew of the inn's charming rooms, which was once the setting for a risky liaison, and I hoped that the name of the inn would impress Michel as a favorable omen.

"You need not worry," the man said, "I will provide for your friend like a prince."

"No luxury is too excessive for the deserving Doctor Nostradamus," I said. "He *is* a prince, a prince among prophets."

A month later I was shocked into remembering just how valueless a court favor can be.

"I rejoice to see you," Michel said dryly, "and if I do not appear to be rejoicing, it is only because I have been bitten by bedbugs and fleas nearly to madness in this month's travel from Salon to Paris."

I gasped. "How can that be possible—I arranged for an acquaintance to ensure the speed and comfort of your journey."

"It was speedy," he grinned wryly, "that is, when I

could find no inn and was forced to continue traveling all night. It was comfortable too, when I slept in the one clean bed of the entire trip, and by then I was ill with chilblains."

His eyes darted beneath the familiar furrowed brow. "But I forgot the discomfort when I arrived in Paris and saw the name of my inn, for surely this is auspicious. And now, here you are to greet me, old friend," he said warmly, grasping my soft upper arm with a hard, taut hand.

"Yes, I can hardly believe my eyes. Of course it has taken many years to entice you, and then you would not come by *my* invitation."

"It is no trifling matter to be summoned to audience with the Queen."

"No doubt she will compensate you handsomely for your troubles, and for your prognostication."

At this he smiled faintly and I recognized the smile I had seen on countless lips; my austere friend was not without an appreciation of profit.

The audience was held the following day. That night we met for supper and at first Michel was reticent to disclose their conversation.

"The Queen wore a wine-red velvet gown; quite impressive."

"Come, come, you are not interested in fashion! Tell me what you spoke about."

He sat pondering for a few moments, then relented. "I see no harm in telling you since court matters reach your ears quickly enough. She inquired after her children, and at her request I had prepared all their horoscopes in advance. They were composed on the basis of natal information sent early the day before; I was awake all night preparing my calculations."

"What did you tell her?"

"I said, 'Your Majesty, all your sons shall be kings.'"

"Excellent remark. But did you really see such a future?"

"In part, yes. I saw that three of the four sons would indeed be crowned King, so I pointed out this beneficent aspect in their horoscopes. What I did not tell her was this: when I consulted my brazier, I saw the stain of early death upon all their faces."

"Death is the germ of your life's work, whether it is physicking or prophesying. I have read *The Prophecies*...may I ask a few questions?"

"Of course, with you Alain I need not mask truth, as I have for strangers. Strangers read my work, you know, and many would like to see me burn for the sheer sport of it."

"You say the world will be destroyed in another two thousand years."

"Which should be of little concern to you."

"You are beginning to sound like one of your own skeptics. Be sincere with me, Michel, for I find myself often wanting to defend your writings, yet there are many questions which keep me silent. For example, you write of a series of anti-Christs which will plague the earth at the end of the twentieth century."

"...and then 'in the year 1999 and seven months, from heaven shall come a terrifying king.'"

"Yes, but what does this mean?"

"Alain, I could have set down in every quatrain the exact time and name of each event, but my honesty would not please everyone. Those who have the Sight will see my intent; those who do not will see it after the tragic events have come to pass—only then will my words have meaning. In this quatrain, the king of terror is not a man but a force, an inferno greater than anyone in our lifetime can imagine. I have no name for this, but its power bade me call it king."

"And what of the passage where you name the city of London and predict a great fire therein? Why are you specific in some quatrains, evasive in others?"

"At times I could give the vision no name; others are veiled for the reasons I have told you. I saw clearly the death of England's great queen, and the impostor who will be executed by their Parliament; and I saw a great fire in the year 1666, though many times the vision is less specific, I only know by the appearance of men and women that these times are far from France and distant in years as well."

"What is to happen in 1792, and shall it be in this land?"

"Because it will be in this land, I chose not to name it. A queen and king of France will be forced to flee in the face of godless insurrection; many will die, and the two will be beheaded, though after this desecration is done, the rule of many lands will change."

"What more have you seen, that you chose not to tell?"

"I have told all, though in words few will understand. I saw a tyrant, of whom I write in the twenty-fourth quatrain of the Second Century. His Aryan reign will be the bloodiest in thousands of years, and he will use my prophecies to persuade many of his followers. I masked the meaning of the quatrains with great care."

I longed to ask him of my own future, but my small life paled before the world events of which he spoke: of plagues and famines, of demagogues and fallen leaders.

"Tell me," I asked, "what of the Queen herself. Did you give her good news?"

"I told the Queen she would realize great power in her lifetime."

"Did she mention your writings?"

"She complimented me on their success, but she added that my well-deserved fame has also brought me into the suspicious eyes of the justice of Paris. She is a follower of the secret arts, but her position affords her dispensation. For the time being I am under her protection, but she warned me not to tarry in Paris lest I fall into the hands of prosecutors."

Following Nostradamus's audience with the King, I did not need coax him for details; he appeared at the door of my room later that same afternoon.

"Back so soon?"

"The audience was brief," he said, seating himself in one of my modest chairs. His face looked drawn, his complexion pale. "The King summoned me only at the Queen's insistence. I expected him to ask an explanation of the quatrain of the golden cage, but he showed no interest; in fact, he seemed indifferent to all my words."

"Knowing the King well, I suspect he only feigned indifference."

"Perhaps so, for I detected concern behind his skeptical smile, as if he was not so coolly dispassionate."

"What was your advice?"

"I spoke of his sons; surprisingly, this made him frown. Perhaps he thinks the Young Lion will be one of his own offspring."

"But it will not?"

"Alain, the King will die in a tourney, on a mock field of battle, and his helmet will blaze golden at the moment of death's mortal blow. Do you believe I could tell King Henri never again to bear a lance?"

Michel's compensation amounted to just over a hundred sovereigns, less than half the money he had invested in his meals and lodging. Then, to his chagrin, at the end of his stay the proprietor of the inn of Saint-Michel placed a tariff into his hand, a bill which should have been paid by my acquaintance, the royal clerk. Even before this embarrassing occurrence, our time spent together lost its savor, for the risk entailed by prolonging his residence in Paris obsessed him; he jumped at the slightest sound, while I endeavored in vain to engage his attention. Then one day I heard from a reliable source that the justice of Paris would soon issue a warrant for his detainment. I reported this to Michel; he departed Paris the following day.

In the early spring of 1558 people milled about the streets fearfully awaiting information about the armies of Phillip of Spain which reportedly were marching toward Paris.

A rumor circulated in the marketplace that the Spanish King intended to sack the city in retaliation for Henri's march into Italy. We feared he was capable. Phillip's forces were terrifying. Assembled with a million ducats borrowed from Anton Fugger of Augsberg and with the backing of Queen Mary of England, the combined arms of Spaniards and mercenaries could indeed demolish us. Our army, led by the Duc de Guise, was still in Italy. King Henri recalled de Guise at once; meanwhile, the city braced herself for siege.

Within the court another view was held by some. Unlike his father Charles V, Phillip hated war. He did not do battle for love of military encounter, but to achieve other ends. On his return from Italy, de Guise besieged Calais; then, with word of this victory preceding him, he marched on toward Paris to confront Phillip's army, only to discover upon his arrival that Paris was out of danger. Phillip, weary of the campaign, had returned to Spain.

It remained only to reaffirm the respective strengths of both kingdoms, acknowledging that Henri's army had the potential of claiming Italy for France, while recognizing Phillip's forces as the potential captors of Paris. It was a show of strength, a brandishing of troops and weaponry, with the result that a treaty was signed on April 2, 1559, at Cateau-Cambrésis, wherein Henri vowed to remain north of the Alps while Phillip agreed to let Henri keep Lorraine and Calais.

The relinquishing of Calais seemed to me a natural product of the contiguity of Spain and France; for Calais had been held by England, Phillip's ally, and England lay distantly across an icy channel. To the eye of common sense, the soil of France and Spain made one flowing vista, broken only by an imaginary line of demarcation.

Coincidentally, I was reflecting on this land bond when someone gave me the news that in recognition of the treaty, Henri would give his daughter Elizabeth to Phillip in marriage and his sister Marguerite to Emanuel Philibert, Duke of Savoy.

Plans for the wedding festival were made in a manner distinctively the King's. One evening after I had attended His Majesty with an hour of light music, he asked me if I remembered the festival celebrating his marriage to Catherine. Before I spoke, I quickly prayed that my answers would be satisfactory, for recently he had chided me for spending too much time with Catherine's own coterie of poets and entertainers.

"I remember it well," I said in a tone that disclosed neither fondness nor distaste.

"As I recall, it was a dreary, stiff affair. But this wedding festival for my daughter and sister shall be long remembered. There are few ways for majesty to display its grandeur. Wars are fought on distant fields, treaties are made inside palace walls. But in this event the dignitaries of many lands and the people of the streets shall all view our splendor."

He raised his eyes toward the gilt ceiling of his chamber and said, "It shall be a festival fit for a hero; befitting of Amadis of Gaul himself."

Exactly as Michel had foretold, the King was felled by a cruel single blow, and yet it was a death which Henri would have chosen.

The power of France now lay in Catherine's hands as Queen Regent, for the Dauphin, François II, was not of age. The Queen's favorites would soon rise to higher positions; soon her real or imagined enemies would be turned out. At this time I knew not on which side of the ledger my name would be.

But within the week I was summoned by a messenger who escorted me to her bedchamber; there, during the early days of mourning, she held informal audience.

I knelt by the bedside and mumbled respectful condolences. Her protruding eyes looked down on me from the high carved bed.

"Rise," she said softly. I stood, my hands dangling awkwardly at my sides; I was nearly faint with anticipation. For years my life had been predictable and I was unaccustomed to such vast uncertainty.

"You were a favorite of my husband," she said in a flat voice that only increased my fear. "Yet I understand that you were not among the favorites of Lady Diane. I welcome you."

I fell to my knees with relief. "I am your servant," I said in a stranger's voice.

"I shall expect more of you than poetry," she said. I stiffened, anticipating some unpleasant intrigue ahead, and her next words were wholly unexpected:

"You are a friend and confidante of Michel de Nostredame."

I braced myself. Would I be asked to conspire against him? But no, she doted upon his advice.

"He is no man of evil intent, as others say. Nostradamus advised me on personal matters, as well as matters of state. Besides his power of foreknowledge, he is a man of shrewd judgment, and I shall guarantee that he is protected. But for my protection, I will expect his counsel in return. Now as his friend and my servant, you will serve as agent between us, to arrange for his sojourns to Paris."

Though grateful to hear this news, my thoughts turned to Michel's last visit to Paris, his ill treatment and inadequate compensation. Perhaps in future I could secure for him a more generous allowance.

"When the people weary of railing against him, he will be honored for his gift," she said, her eyes narrowing, "and such a man must be my ally."

Brightened by the prospect of seeing him again, I wrote an exuberant letter; in it I assured him of the Queen's protection and the promise of security and comfort in his old age. His reply was handed me by my new assistant some six weeks later:

I appreciate your effort on my behalf; however, you must inform the Queen that my health fails. As a physician, I know that for the severe pain in my joints and for the pressure of bodily fluids which distend my body like a swollen river, there is no relief but death. For this eventuality I am preparing my will.

Also, while royal patronage is an honor, it is in practice small consolation for my painful life. The daily reality is filled with *cabans,* ignorant hordes who call after me "filthy devil's pen" or "cursed Jew." Thus I may be honored by the Queen; meanwhile the masses detest me. As for my work, this has been imparted to my remarkable student, de Chavigny; my secrets shall rest in his discreet hands.

I implore you to advise the Queen of my physical debility so she may not expect me to travel to and fro. As for remuneration, I am well set out due to the revenue from my writings. Also my wife possesses a substantial estate.

I am, however, at the Queen's disposal—in Salon, or by post. My best wishes for your continued health and prosperity.

M.N.

The Queen listened to my paraphrase of his letter, which I sweetened somewhat to dilute his acerbic words. She accepted his decline with equanimity, but this did not mean she would relinquish her claim to Michel's services.

"Then we shall travel to his home," she said calmly. "Where does he reside?"

"In Salon, Your Highness," I replied, incredulous at the idea of an official journey to the south of France, replete with pomp and attendants—all for a few hours in the gloomy, disheveled study of Michel de Nostredame.

"This sojourn will benefit my son, for I intended a tour of the provinces to debut him before his countrymen. Speak to my secretary and make sure Salon is included in our itinerary; a one-day delay in the progression, only."

But five years elapsed before we made the royal progression. The tour was delayed, of course, for the poor health of François II would not allow it; indeed, he died less than two years after his father's death, making a widow of his young bride, Mary of the Scots. This brought his brother Charles in line for the throne. He was proclaimed Charles IX and the tour at last was scheduled for the following year.

I found myself doing double duty, helping with the details of planning the progression, and also involved in the somber task of disposing of my Uncle Léon's estate. My parents had died a few years before, but due to the many years which had elapsed since I had last seen them, their loss affected me less deeply than the death of my shrewd and dignified uncle, who had advised me, and I him, until his final days.

When I was informed of his considerable debts, I reflected that my information over the years may have caused him to give loans to the wrong clients. Now I, his heir, would pay for such misdirection. After selling off his lodgings and furnishings to settle his debts, I was left with only a small sum, plus his library, and that I had refused to sell.

I was suddenly faced with mortality, now that my elder relative no longer provided a more wrinkled contrast. Thus it was, when I wrote to inform Michel of the progression, I told him of my small inheritance and my desire to leave Paris and return to the southern land of my birth. In his reply, he suggested that I purchase a small home near his; with this in mind, I made arrangements for the property he recommended and began to resolve unfinished business in the city which for forty years had provided my livelihood.

I left Paris with one reluctance, that my son would never know me. Yet the Lady Yvette was one of the few who acknowledged my departure; in exchange for beauty, time had made her heart grow kind.

The royal entourage assembled and we began our southward journey. Salon was my destination but until we reached it, I would serve the Queen Regent one last time. This was not my first progression, for I had accompanied Henri to Rouen, Tours and Lyons many years before, when Diane rode beneath the emblem of the crescent moon and Catherine followed in the dusk. But now the Lady Diane had been deposed, the jewels Henri had bestowed on her were taken away, and Catherine rode at the fore, powerful in her widowhood. For assurance of the futures of her children we turned from the main road and toward Salon.

I left the entourage at the crossroads unpacking mules to erect shelter for the night. With no difficulty I located Michel's home again. I struck the clapper on his door and waited; soon a young boy appeared at the doorway. This must be César, I thought. He greatly resembled his father when Michel was the dark, slim boy who had walked with me in the fields of Saint-Rémy, and I was sad to think of a lifetime nearly spent.

"Come in, Alain, come in!" I heard an irritated voice call from across the room. I stepped inside to see Michel lying on a cot by the fire, bundled in blankets. He was buried in wool except for his face and hands, which were puffed and moist with perspiration. I must have looked aghast.

"I did not realize you were so ill," I stammered, not knowing whether to embrace him, for I might increase his pain. I stood uneasily in the center of the stifling room.

"Come close, Alain, do not be offended by my gruffness. To some of us it comes with age."

"But we are the same age," I protested.

". . . with age, pain and the aggravation of a large family." He smiled then and I saw that his still-bright eyes looked with affection upon the five children nearby. I noticed, too, that his tenderest glance lingered on the face of his daughter, Madeleine. He introduced me to them, then said, "Now leave us for a time. A man's conversation requires peace and quiet."

I accustomed myself to his distended body and to his painful nervous spasms. We talked until late in the night and he told of his fear of releasing hold on life and his place at the head of his family. Michel worried lest Madeleine should not be provided a proper dowry, and he went into great detail about the provisions of his will.

"I am a wealthy man," he said. "My estate consists of over two thousand ecus, as well as property. These gems I have set aside for my daughter."

I did not disclose my thoughts, of how the daughter bore not only the name of his first wife but also her fragile radiance.

"She cannot follow my direction and know the treasures granted to my eyes, for she is a woman and in these times such understanding would condemn her to a wretched, lonely life. Yet I can give her these, to secure her future. All but this one," he said, lifting a violet stone from the coffer, "for it must accompany me to my grave. Amethyst was the gem favored by Egyptians for safely conducting the souls of the dead."

"Do you foresee the time of your death?" I asked.

"It draws near. I have been apprised and have noted the date on my ephemeris."

I found our conversation melancholy, but since it was his wish to discuss death and wills, I would not deny him this and asked, "What of your other children, your wife, your eldest son César?"

"They have been provided for though César worries me. I shall leave him my ring and astrolabe, besides an inheritance. Yet the thing of greatest value which I can give my son must be withheld. I fear he is not of a serious nature and that my books and their secrets could be misused. Therefore I have arranged for all volumes in my library to be sealed away until the three boys have reached maturity; only then will Anne decide which one is to inherit them."

"The dire events you have seen," I began, "is there no hope for mankind? Can we not redeem ourselves— and if not, what is the purpose of prophecy?"

"I once feared to become another Jeremiah. It is true that in my old age I now lament and pray that many of my predictions will not unfold."

"Why should some be realized and not others?" I asked.

"Let me tell you the difference between foreknowledge and prophecy. The Book of Corinthians says 'we know in part and we prophesy in part.' I have been granted a vision of those events which may come to pass if the pattern of destiny is not altered. My vision of future time is not one of destination, but only of direction. Do you remember the small green snake we tossed into the air one day, long ago, in Saint-Rémy? We were certain it would land on the ground, yet we found it high in a tree. Mankind possesses a greater power: the will and the strength to alter his own course."

Anne then tapped softly on the door to remind us of the hour.

"Help me to the study before you go," he said. "I shall sleep there tonight, so the Queen will not have to watch me struggle down these stairs tomorrow. I shall give the consultation in my chamber."

At the top of the stairway we embraced, and I closed the door behind him.

We had but three seasons together to savor our renewed friendship, for early in the month of July of 1566
he was found collapsed by his desk; nearby was an
ephemeris, with that very day marked with a cross. De
Chavigny, Michel's student, helped the widow arrange
Michel's papers, but when he requested his teacher's
library, the provisions of the will forbade it.

I was present at the reading of the will and it was
as Michel had told me, with one curious amendment:
if his wife, Anne, were to bear a posthumous child, he
included a revised table for the apportioning of his es-
tates and there was another supplement if the theo-
retical posthumous birth proved to be twins. Of course,
this did not occur and so the original will was executed.

Thus we are protective of our lineage, that our issue
shall survive.

But I expect to live a good while longer even though
no arcane wisdom assures me of this, for I am not a
man given to visions. Yet sometimes I wish it were so.
Because I have often thought of Michel de Nostredame
and me as the obverse and reverse sides of a coin. His
was a defiant face before the world, famous and infa-
mous in his own time; mine was a face hidden behind
great men and women. Michel was a prophet who wrote
in a poet's quatrains, and I a poet who captured small
joys and sorrows.

If I had his vision and could see the future, would I
find a change of position on the coin? Would my poetry
live on and the name of Nostradamus be forgotten?

AUTHOR'S NOTE

I began the research and writing of *Vagabond Prophet* ten years ago as a graduate student in History of Religions at UCLA. At first I was unsure of my position regarding Nostradamus. Was he authentic or fraudulent?—was he a prophet whose predictions have since been validated by events or was he merely the perpetrator of the longest-running hoax in history?

I concluded that the durability of *The Prophecies of Michel de Nostredame* seems less remarkable (and less likely to have been conceived as a hoax) when it is compared to other "prophetic" material such as the *I Ching* and the pictorial Tarot, for all three share a like quality: a universal and inclusive imagery which invites interpretation.

I have taken the position that Nostradamus was authentic and urged on by an inner sense or purpose, though not always clear about his goal and thus forced to wander like a vagabond in his quest for the unknown. This position has allowed me to consider what manner of studies and mystical experiences might have led to his vision and to the writing of *The Prophecies*. This concern and an interest in the influence of the times in which he lived—the French Renaissance—suggested to me that the story could best be told from the viewpoint of one who would observe Nostradamus with a sympathetic and yet, occasionally, a cynical eye. For this reason the narrator is Alain Saint-Germain, a fictional sixteenth-century urban man whose characteristics are drawn in part from accounts of his younger "contemporary," the poet Pierre Ronsard.

Though I have exercised the novelist's license to create this secondary character and other minor characters who enable the telling of the tale, I have tried to be faithful to the details known of Nostradamus's life. With the exception of his birth and death, however, many other dates traditionally assigned to his life are disputed by students of the subject. The timetable that follows shows the general framework upon which *Vagabond Prophet* was based.

Guiding me further in this effort were the legends transmitted across four centuries, including the prognostication of Florinville's suckling pig and Nostradamus's vision of Felix Peretti in his later position as Pope Sixtus V. I have been aided, also, by descriptions of the appearance of Michel de Nostredame and of his character as "idealistic" and "taciturn except when his interest was aroused," as the traditional account attributed to his student, de Chavigny, describes him.

Just as there are conflicting details concerning Michel de Nostredame's life, so are the quatrains amenable to often conflicting and sometimes wildly imaginative interpretations. It is widely known that Adolf Hitler's minister of propaganda, Joseph Goebbels, used "interpretations" of the quatrains in an attempt to persuade the people of occupied France that the coming of the Third Reich was predestined. Recent popular editions of the quatrains, such as Erika Cheetham's *The Prophecies of Nostradamus* (London: Neville Spearman, Ltd., 1973; now in a Perigee edition), besides the traditional interpretations of the quatrains—which include such events as the French Revolution and the beheadings of Louis XVI, Marie Antoinette and Madame duBarry, as well as the great fire of London and the rise and fall of Napoleon—offer other explanations of interest to the twentieth-century reader, and allude to the Kennedy brothers, the Polaris submarine, the skyscrapers of New York City.

When earlier interpreters are compared with Cheetham, one expects to find variations, depending on the time and concerns of the writer. Curiously, while Cheetham offers that the word "hister" (or Ister) in verse twenty-four of the Second Century of *The Prophecies* means "Hitler," an earlier translator/commentator, Henry Roberts, did not make this connection, though he was writing in the late 1940s. Perhaps Roberts considered the interpretation as too great a stretch of credulity, since "Hister" *is* the name of a river in Germany; perhaps he merely failed to see the obvious, though the name "Hitler" could hardly have been far from his mind at the time he was writing, and many of his other comments refer to incidents of the Second World War.

Most translators/interpreters of *The Prophecies* use a variety of deciphering methods to impart a prophetic meaning to Nostradamus's quatrains, but a similar method can be used to foreshorten Nostradamus's alleged vision of the far future. In the 1979 edition of *The Prophecies and Enigmas of Nostradamus* by Liberte E. LeVert (pseudonym of science fiction writer E. F. Bleiler), the author argues that many of the quatrains in *Les Prophéties* can be explained as symbolic descriptions of events during or slightly before the time in which Nostradamus was writing. LeVert suggests that the title word "prophecy" would not have been taken as literally as readers take it today. Moreover, LeVert concludes that many of the quatrains were conscious commercial efforts and that certain of the cryptic poems were penned to earn him the favor of the court.

Though LeVert may be correct, his "reductio" depends upon the same logic of symbolic deciphering as that used by others like Cheetham and Roberts. The case, it appears, is not closed. Nor is it likely to be, for the legacy of Nostradamus cannot easily be dismissed with a single set of interpretations. And if the past is an indication, no doubt the quatrains will continue to be interpreted, and accepted as prophecy, by future generations.

Allene Symons
New York City
February, 1983

CHRONOLOGY

- Concordat; Leo X grants François I permission to appoint bishops and abbots (1516)

Michel de Nostredame born in Saint-Rémy de Provence (1503)

- Sorbonne condemns Martin Luther as a heretic (1521)

Michel attends school in Avignon (1520–22?)

- Duke of Bourbon attempts to seize Provence; fails (1524)

Michel studies at the college of medicine, Montpellier (1523–25?)

- Capture of Milan fails; François I is confined in Alcazar prison in Madrid (1525)

Michel leaves Montpellier, travels and ministers to victims of the plague (1525–29?)

- François I offers his two sons as hostages to secure his release (1526)

Michel returns to Montpellier, receives doctorate, teaches on faculty (1529–32)

- After four years (1529) princes are free; Prince Henri is betrothed to Catherine de Medici (1533)

Michel leaves Montpellier and resumes his travels in France (1532–34)

- Huguenot presence increases in Southern France; "placardists" outrage the Paris court (1534)

Michel establishes residence in Agen, with César Scaliger as his patron. He marries (1534) has two children, but his family dies of pestilence; he is accused of heresy (1538)

- The Dauphin dies after a tennis match; poison is suspected (1536)

Michel travels, possibly to Italy as well as in France; lives briefly in Lyons, Aix, and Marseilles. Marries, lives in Salon (1547)

- François I dies at age fifty-three; his son Henri inherits the crown (1547)

First of Michel de Nostredame's almanacs published (1550)

- Henri II arranges marriage of son François to Mary Stuart of Scotland (1558)

Traicté des Fardemens published (1554)

- (1558) Charles V abdicates; the Crown of the Holy Roman Empire passes to his brother Ferdinand, and his son Phillip becomes King of the Spanish Dominions; Protestants (according to account of Sorzano) number 400,000 and are now called "Calvinists"

First edition of *Le Prophéties* (incomplete) (1555) Michel summoned to Paris by Catherine de Medici (1556)

- Henri II dies accidentally in a joust at a wedding celebration (1559)

Complete edition of *Le Prophéties* (ten centuries) published (1558)

- The Dauphin becomes François II, (1559) but dies within a year (1560)

Charles IX and his mother Catherine de Medici visit Nostradamus in Salon (1565)

Michel de Nostredame dies on July 1, 1566, at the age of 63

BIBLIOGRAPHY

Batiffol, Louis. *The Century of the Renaissance in France*. Trans. by E. F. Buckley. New York: G. P. Putnam's Sons, 1916.

Bishop, Morris. *Ronsard: Prince of Poets*. London: Oxford University Press, 1940.

Boman, Thorleif. *Hebrew Thought Compared with Greek*. Library of History and Doctrine. Philadelphia: Westminster Press, 1954–1960.

Cheetham, Erika (Ed. and Trans.). *The Prophecies of Nostradamus*. London: Neville Spearman, Ltd., 1973.

Chomarat, Michel. *Nostradamus Entre Rhone et Saone*. Lyons: Ger Editeur, 1971.

Crouzet, François. *Nostradamus Poète Français*. Paris: Julliard, 1973.

Febvre, Lucien. *Life in Renaissance France*. Ed. and Trans. by Marion Rothstein. Cambridge: Harvard University Press, 1977.

Leoni, Edgar. *Nostradamus: Life and Literature*. Smithtown, N.Y.: Exposition Press, 1961.

LeVert, Liberte E. *The Prophecies and Enigmas of Nostradamus*. Glen Rock, N.J.: Firebell Books, 1979.

Roberts, Henry C. (Ed., Interp. and Trans.). *The Complete Prophecies of Nostradamus*. Great Neck, N.Y.: Nostradamus, Inc., 1947.

Strong, Roy C. *Splendor at Court*. Boston: Houghton Mifflin Co., 1973.

Wiley, W. L. *The Gentlemen of Renaissance France*. Cambridge: Harvard University Press, 1954.

THE CONCISE COLUMBIA ENCYCLOPEDIA

THE COLUMBIA UNIVERSITY PRESS

A new, comprehensive, and authoritative, one-volume encyclopedia of biographies, facts and information for everyday use in the 80's. Written under the guidance of a distinguished panel of scholars in every field, THE CONCISE COLUMBIA ENCYCLOPEDIA is the product of years of careful research and planning to make an encyclopedia's worth of information available in one volume which is small enough to take anywhere!

- Over 15,000 entries covering every field of information
- Over 3,000 articles on up-to-date scientific and technical subjects—from computers to robotics and quarks
- Broad coverage of people and topics of contemporary importance—from Sandra Day O'Connor and Luciano Pavarotti to genetic engineering and herpes simplex
- Over 5,000 biographies of notable men and women, past and present
- Illustrations, diagrams, charts, national and regional maps
- A 16-page world atlas of political and topographical maps
- Over 50,000 cross references to additional information
- Pronunciation guide for difficult names and words
- Metric equivalents for all measurements
- Plus special tables listing U.S. presidents, Supreme Court justices, popes, prime ministers, rulers, royal dynasties, national parks, theaters, orchestras, languages, planets, elements—and much more!

An AVON Trade Paperback   63396-5/$14.95

THE POWERFUL NEW BESTSELLER
BY THE AUTHOR OF
BREAD UPON THE WATER AND
RICH MAN POOR MAN

IRWIN SHAW
ACCEPTABLE LOSSES

A death threat in the middle of the night
shatters the life of successful literary agent
Roger Damon. Who is his caller?
And why does he want to kill Damon?

"Looking into the face of death is obviously what
Roger Damon's experience is about...The terror
provoked by his mysterious enemy...cleverly
plotted and absorbing." *The New York Times*

"ACCEPTABLE LOSSES is everything we
expect out of Irwin Shaw." *Chicago Tribune*

"The suspense of a thriller...the intimacy
of a character study...in a fast-paced
narrative." *The New York Times Book Review*

An AVON Paperback **64162-3/$3.95**